TRUE IDENTITY

The Lost and Found Series
Book One

Amanda Mackey

Limitless Publishing, LLC
Kailua, HI 96734
www.limitlesspublishing.com

Formatting: Limitless Publishing

ISBN-13: 978-1-64034-173-9
ISBN-10: 1-64034-173-0

Chapter One

Mackenzie

My two week break officially ended the moment I walked through the doors of University Hospital in Ann Arbor, Michigan. My place of employment was in pandemonium. There would be no easing into the day. It went from zero to chaotic in ten seconds flat without giving me time to take a much needed deep breath. I worked in ICU, which on a good day, bordered on mildly chaotic. Today would be much worse.

I likened it to stepping into a tornado. Outside the doors lay the *eye of the storm*. Eerily calm, yet ripe with tense anticipation of the impending carnage. You know you have to go through it, but falter at the threshold nonetheless, wondering what lies within its clutches.

Doctors and nurses blew through with critical agendas, speaking in codes only reserved for the medical profession. My brain switched into high gear, adrenalin providing me with the kick I'd need to function at warp speed as the doors to outside normality shut behind me.

"Mac! You're back. Tell me later about your holiday. Right now we've got a Code Blue in room five. Throw your bag into the nurse's station and let's go."

I could have about turned and stalked out, pretending I still had another week of vacation left, but it wasn't in my nature as a nurse to turn my back on sick patients. Code Blue had everyone running. Death loomed. Days like this tested us to our core. We'd all trained for it. It was a buzz like no other.

Flashes of blue uniforms scurried past us like roaches to food scraps. Charlotte, my fellow nurse and friend, looked stressed as I tossed my bag on the bottom shelf of the oblong work desk amongst the other clutter, and hurried down the hall, seizing the stethoscope she held out.

"An old guy. Brought in yesterday. Unconscious. Found by his wife, slumped on the lounge chair. At first he appeared asleep, but as time went on, she tried to wake him. When he didn't respond, she called 911. It's not looking good."

She puffed as she spoke, attempting to give me a rundown. I struggled to keep up as we forced our way past a food trolley and a doctor pushing a middle-aged man in a wheelchair.

Lucky for me I'd dressed in my navy scrubs prior to leaving home. Some staff changed here and kept clothes in their lockers. I found it easier to be prepared. On days like today I didn't need to waste valuable time.

I followed Charlotte into the patient's room, where two doctors and nurses hovered.

Chase Andrews and Chris Hartley had the paddles out. Chase situated them on the sunken, bony chest of the elderly man. Chris set the voltage. The two nurses, Debbie and Jacinta, glanced at us with grim faces. Jacinta scribbled something down on a clipboard while Debbie, whose shift I took over, stood by and watched, waiting on further instruction if needed. There were too many people in the room, but with a Code Blue, it didn't matter. Everyone available assisted.

"Clear!" cried Chase as he administered the voltage, the patient's saggy torso arching off the bed.

The heart monitor had flat-lined and the single drone of the machine echoed a sound we were all used to, but one we all loathed.

I whispered to Charlotte, "Where's his wife?"

"She went home last night to rest so she could return a little later. We've called her and she's on her way."

Chase barked out again and gave more voltage to the man. The whine of the machine remained unchanged. Mortality stared us all in the face.

Inching over to Jacinta, I held my hand out for the clipboard and scanned it when she gave it to me.

Mr. William Morris. Aged 87. History of angina. In 2010 he'd had a quadruple bypass. Everything else appeared normal.

It all seemed cut and dry to me, but Chase didn't look ready to call it yet. My heart went out to his wife, whom if Mr. Morris didn't pull through, would never get to say her goodbyes. No matter the age, it always left a traumatic scar. I'd consoled many family members after they'd received the devastating news. Not an easy task, but part of our job. I tried not to take it home with me, and most times I could distance myself. Children were the hardest though, and they were usually the ones I lost sleep over.

I'd spent twelve months in the children's ward. For the most part it remained upbeat and fun with clowns and other entertainers calling in to brighten the sick kids' days. Then there were the times after car accidents, fatal diseases, or domestic violence attacks when the weight of my job really dragged me down. Young lives taken too soon. Shattered parents and siblings. The defining, horrific moment of impact when lives changed irreparably. Questions unanswered. What ifs. It all came with the territory.

Charlotte disappeared and returned with a syringe of epinephrine, which she began injecting into the cannula. I felt helpless standing there watching but no one had asked me for anything. I guess I acted as a backup, if needed.

Everyone waited with bated breath for the familiar beep, beep of the machine, but it never came, and Chase called it twenty minutes later at 8:17 a.m.

A thick blanket of morbidity covered the room while we inhaled, and then we were all being given orders on the exhale. Emotions had to be kept in-check. We all had to do it in order to cope with the death we witnessed daily. Our psyches acted accordingly. It hadn't always been easy. First weeks and months on the job were sink or swim for some. The toughest survived. At the end of the day we were all human, and I'd be lying if I said each and every doctor and nurse hadn't been affected greatly by at least one incident while working.

"Mackenzie, can you call down to the morgue and let them know they have a pickup? Char, hang around for when Mrs. Morris arrives, and take her to the lounge and get her a cup of coffee and anything else she needs. Call other family if you have to."

Chase covered Mr. Morris with an overly starched sheet and began walking out as if a man hadn't just lost his life. Chris cleared away the paddles and followed Chase into the hallway. Debbie shook her head and walked out silently with her eyes downcast, and Jacinta began removing the cannula, adjusting the sheet so she could access his arm without disturbing his covered face.

I made my way back to the nurse's station and called the morgue. Back to business as normal. Cue, the very real life of medical staff. With Debbie now being on vacation and me taking over from her, I had a new patient to take care of. I wasn't sure who I had yet, but when I saw her loitering just shy of the nurse's desk, I closed the gap.

"How you holding up?" I asked. She'd only been with us for six months. Her ability to disengage from loss wasn't as well-formed as mine. After completing her training and internship, she'd started with us as a full-time employee. Being young, she had a lot to learn, but everyone loved her friendly personality.

We would miss her while she visited her ill mother in Canada.

Her eyes were glassy, but there were no fallen tears. "I'm all right. I try not to let death get to me, but it's hard, you know? Especially with Mom being diagnosed with multiple sclerosis."

Resting a comforting hand on her shoulder, I squeezed. "I do know, and if you want to call me tonight before you leave in the morning and chat about it, I'll be home."

Her mom was in her mid-fifties and had MS. Her motor skills were failing, so Debbie wanted to go and help her. While she was there, she would organize home nursing to make it easier. My heart went out to my colleague. I'd seen my fair share of the debilitating effects of advanced MS. Some patients went downhill rapidly after diagnosis, and others lived with it more tolerably for longer.

Smiling, she said, "Thanks, but I'll be fine. Nothing a good bottle of wine and my boyfriend giving me a neck massage won't fix."

I scoffed in jest. "Half your luck! Nick's never given me a massage. I've hinted often enough, but I think he has selective hearing."

We'd been dating and living together for two years. As an investment banker, he worked a lot. Actually *a lot* was too mild. He *always* worked. If he wasn't at the bank, he worked from home after hours. It had almost always been that way, and listening to Debbie tell me about her attentive partner drove home the very real fact that Nick and I hadn't been intimate for the last couple of months.

With my shifts changing regularly and Nick always too tired, sex just didn't happen. It had become routine to both of us. I had day shifts for the next couple of weeks, but then I'd have to wait for the new roster.

Handing me a file and drawing me to the present, Debbie replied, "You need to walk away, Mac. There are plenty of guys out there who would be only too willing to dote on you."

I'd had this conversation with her and Charlotte before, but to be honest, Nick was comfortable. I'd grown used to the way things were, even if I did secretly yearn for more. The unknown frightened me. At twenty-seven, I shouldn't have been such a wuss, but sometimes *better the devil you know*, right?

"Pfft. You're just saying that because you're my friend. Why haven 't any ever shown up in my life?"

"Well, your new patient is a hottie." She pointed at the file. "He's been in an induced coma, but girl, mmm, he's fine. I wish he'd open his eyes so I could see what color they are, but judging by his ebony hair, I'm guessing a rich brown. Hopefully he'll wake up soon. He's being weaned off the drugs."

And just like that, Debbie had forgotten about her grief over losing old Mr. Morris. She now blushed.

"You're trouble, you know that? Go on home to that fine boyfriend of yours and don't think about this place for the next couple of weeks. I hope your mom will be okay. Keep us posted, okay?"

Giving her a hug, I watched her walk away before strolling to the room of my new patient.

Chapter Two

Mac

I wasn't sure what to expect when I pushed through the door into room three, but the hulk of a man with arms busting out of the generous hospital gown wasn't it.

Debbie had been on the mark. Wow! Impressive didn't begin to describe him. A thick neck led to a face that could only be labeled as rugged with a hint of danger. The visible exterior held no femininity. Tanned and slightly hardened skin, as if weathered from the sun, covered a square face. His nose had character with its ruler straight bridge. A short, dark military-style cut, which looked like it had grown out some, stood at attention like a worn brush. I took pause just inside the door to stare at the masterpiece. My wandering eyes led me to covet his black, stark eyelashes that rested way too still. What lay beyond? Was Debbie correct in her assumption of deep, dusky eyes? Or would they be the color of a turbulent sea? There was no oxygen mask present, which meant he breathed on his own, so I had a front row seat to the pièce de résistance. His mouth! Lord have mercy. May I burn in hell for the instant image of those decadent lips eliciting shivers to erupt all over my skin as they trail-blazed unchartered pathways all over me. I mentally chastised myself as I shuffled closer. My heart stuttered and almost stalled in my chest. A lancing pain shot diagonally through it and into my abdomen, momentary but intense. Not an *I'm having a heart attack* kind of pain, but more of a stunned stupid, intrinsic reaction from every cell in my body. My hormones kicked into gear. I'd just stepped into Narnia. A fictional world within my world. No man so fine had ever appeared in my ICU, and now that he had, I bumbled like an idiot.

Good God, I had a job to do, and it didn't involve ogling a sick man, no matter how physically appealing he was.

Opening his file, a nurse had scribbled John Doe as his name. The guy must have been without ID. Injuries included a single gunshot wound to the chest, narrowly missing his heart. Also internal cranial bleeding, which had stabilized. He'd been removed from assisted breathing yesterday, which proved hopeful for his recovery. Given his injuries, luck played a part in him not being in the morgue with old Mr. Morris. Perhaps his tough exterior infiltrated inwards. He looked like a man who could take a beating and then some. Battle hardened.

I inched closer, unable to help myself, deciding to break the silence and treat him like any other patient. After all, some coma patients could hear, but not move or communicate.

"Hi, John Doe. I'm Mackenzie. Everyone calls me Mac because, well…Mackenzie is just too much of a mouthful."

My stethoscope still hung around my neck, so I proceeded to check his pulse, only to be rattled further by the smoothness of his wrist as I listened to the steady *thrump* of his blood being pushed through his veins. My fingers lingered longer than necessary, but I gave myself the rare luxury of indulging in the discreet transgression.

"You don't look like a John. You look more like a Harley. You own a motorbike?" His pulse beat normally, so I picked up his chart at the end of the bed and jotted down some numbers before placing it back again.

Padding to stand back at his side, I afforded his face a longer glance, hoping he could at least hear the sound of my voice. "So, what's your story, Harley? Who are you really, and what are you doing in my ICU? Surely you must have family looking for you. A girlfriend or wife? You've been here a week and nobody has reported you missing. Technically, you don't exist. You're a ghost."

Scrutinizing him enabled me to take in all his adequate features. "Who shot you? Are you wanted by criminals or were you in the wrong place at the wrong time?"

If I wasn't aware of a bullet hole covered up by the blankets, I'd merely think he was taking a nap. There were no other wounds visible. He obviously hadn't been beaten up prior to the shooting. Cranial bleeding? Maybe the back of his head had suffered blunt force trauma. I couldn't tell front on.

"You're going to get sick of me rambling all day, but it helps me as much as it helps you. If you're real lucky, I may even sing for you."

I adored singing. I'd been doing it since I could remember. Not in front of an audience though, just around friends and family. People remarked I should enter into talent competitions, but I had no desire to take it further. I loved my job as a nurse, and couldn't imagine doing anything else. Plus, the thought of being in front of a crowd singing made me sick to my stomach. I'd never been an attention seeker. More of a *hide in the background* type girl.

On autopilot, I began humming a tune as I went about hooking up another fluid bag, noticing his present one was all but empty. I then checked the equipment and machines to make sure they were all working properly. I also added another blanket to the top of him. The air conditioning kept everything cool. Most *awake* patients complained of being cold, so I had to assume he was the same, while not being able to communicate.

I broke into song while I executed my routine, singing Rhianna's "Work." It was fitting for the moment. Losing myself in the words, the time sped by, and before long, the door opened and my relief nurse came in, signaling break time.

"Hey Mac. Belt it out, girl! Wow! That voice gives me goosebumps."

"Hahaha, yeah right, Karen. Maybe it's the acoustics in here making me sound better than I actually am."

"Oh listen to you, always so modest. I'm sure

Mr. Hunk here is enjoying it too." She gazed wistfully at Harley, causing me to chuckle.

"I've re-named John Doe here Harley. I figure he needed to be called something. Harley fits, don't you think?"

Pondering on it for a moment, she smiled. "Actually, yeah, it does. Harley it is, then. Now you run along and get a coffee and some food and I'll keep an eye on the Greek god, here." Winking at me, she shooed me out.

I bet her day just got a whole lot better. Mine had.

Chapter Three

Harley

I had to be dead. An angel sang. Her voice filtered through my consciousness and liquefied every cell. The cherub quality infiltrated my consuming darkness, giving me a buoy to latch onto before I drowned in the black ocean of nothing.

Lost. Unseeing. Unmoving. Stuck somewhere I couldn't name. Neither here nor there. Up or down? It couldn't tell. I was but a thought. No body, just awareness. Alert to her sound, with no mistaking the femininity of her tone. And the words, although jumbled, I understood.

Like a warm cocoon, I was wrapped up in every syllable. Every pitch and dip. The inflection oozed through me and I, through it, as if we were one and the same. I grew wings and soared on the notes. I wanted to cling to them and never let go.

While I reflected, questions popped up. Had I led a good life? What did I do? Had I been married with children? A criminal or a good, clean man? As much as my memory evaded me, I did know I was male. Without a doubt. An inherent knowing. Different from the voice, as if the polar opposite. Another tidbit for me to cling to.

The angel's voice changed and then stopped. *No, I cried out into the crevasse. Don't stop. Please. I need to hear you. Don't leave me in the dark with no sound.*

But then voices began again. Two this time. Distinctly different. My angel's was harmonious. Lush. The other one fell deeper. Less enthralling.

Words were announced which I could understand. "I've re-named John Doe here Harley…"

Me? John Doe? Something about it sounded off, like it didn't fit. But then was Harley any better? Maybe. I filed it away, clinging to further sounds.

More words cut into my coffin of black. "Now you run along…I'll keep an eye on the Greek god, here."

The deep voice. Footsteps? Was my angel leaving? Why? No. She couldn't!

Stay! Angel. Whoever you are. I'm begging you. I don't want someone else. I want you. You sound nice. Soothing. I don't like the new voice.

Panic gave me the sensation of plummeting. Freefalling with no parachute. It was eerily quiet. No whooshing sounds rushing past me like there would be if I were jumping from a plane. No wind. Nothing. Just a feeling like my stomach had been left somewhere higher up.

And then without warning, I jerked as if hitting the bottom. I was heavy. Dense. Aware of my arms and legs weighing me down. In fact, my whole body had turned to lead.

Other sounds came to me. A beeping sound. Shuffling. Trying to move my limbs met with impenetrable resistance. Paralysis. My equilibrium had returned. With all the effort I could muster, I attempted to move a finger, but the weight of one digit equated to a gross ton.

I felt more human than I had when I'd been floating. As if my body were real now and not a figment of my imagination.

"Hello, Harley. I'm Karen. Boy, Mac sure is lucky having you as her patient. Damn. We haven't had anyone as fine as you in a long time. If ever." Karen loitered close by, her low voice increasing in volume. Did I know her? She called me Mac's patient. Where had I fallen to? Another part of heaven? A hospital in the sky? Nothing rang true for me.

"We get a lot of old men around here. Not that there is anything wrong with that, but you've brought with you a welcome change of scenery. Yes, indeed."

Trying to answer, I couldn't speak. This alternate universe I found myself in began to frighten the hell out of me. How could I hear talking and the damn beeping sound, but my body wouldn't move? My eyes were fused shut, and if I even had a mouth, it felt like a golf ball had lodged in the base of my throat.

"You'll really like Mac. She's as sweet as they come. A darn good nurse too. If anyone can make you better, it's her. She's been with this hospital as long as I have. Five years. Mightn't seem like much, but in this line of work, it's a lifetime."

My ears pricked up at the name of my singing angel. She hadn't left permanently. That meant she'd return.

As much as I preferred Mac's voice to Karen's, just having someone speaking brought with it a certain level of comfort. To not be alone. For the next little while, I focused on words only, listening to idle chatter. It eventually tipped me back into obscurity.

Chapter Four

Mac

After a marathon day at the hospital, I made it home around six p.m., thankful while on holidays, I'd prepared a few meals and stuck them in the freezer. It would merely be a matter of thawing and heating.

After being on my feet for hours, I tossed my shoes aside at the front door of the apartment I shared with Nick.

Harley flooded my mind. The mystery surrounding him made me want to find out about his life. Where did he live? What did he do for a living? Without any information I couldn't do much. I hated not knowing all the facts. My nature was to help others, but how could you help someone who had no identity? A handsome guy with no ID? Who didn't carry a cell or wallet? Had he been robbed before being shot? That made sense. Perhaps the assailants had needed drug money and taken anything they could find.

No use mulling over it. When the guy woke up we'd know more.

Nick's motorbike had been parked in the visitor's lot, not far from our garage, which he couldn't use, as we only had space for my car. It wasn't a meaty bike, but more of a scooter on steroids. An embarrassment really, but he believed in saving every buck wherever he could, including fuel costs. The thing ran on vapors.

"Nick?" I called, noticing the living room empty.

I didn't expect him to be sitting idly, watching the television, or helping to do any of the chores, so I let my feet lead me toward our bedroom on autopilot.

The door was wide open and sure enough, Nick had his back to me, hunched over his laptop.

He barely even glanced up as I walked in and stood beside him. "Did you hear me come home?"

"Hmm?" he asked, distracted by the flurry of numbers on his screen.

Shaking my head, I turned around. "Never mind. Dinner will be ready in a bit. I'm going to shower and change."

He mumbled something and I left him to it, remembering Debbie's words. *You need to walk away, Mac.*

There had to be more to life, surely. More to a relationship. My boyfriend treated me as if I were invisible. Housemate would be a better term because that's what we had become. Two ships passing in the night. Strangers living under the same roof who barely conversed anymore.

I bet if Harley woke up, he'd have plenty to say.

And there went my brain, thinking about him again. Mystery man. Spending the whole day singing and talking with a comatose male had been far more enjoyable than five minutes in Nick's company. I really needed to reassess my life. Living alone would be no different than my current situation. I needed to take the plunge, comfortable or not.

Pulling some sweatpants and a tank from my drawers, I eased into the bathroom, shutting the door on my mute boyfriend before turning up the heat to damn near scalding.

Sheesh. When had we last gone out to dinner or watched a movie? Things that normal couples do. We may as well be living apart, because the distance between us at present measured larger than the Grand Canyon. He never asked about my day, and I'd given up long ago attempting to get more than a couple of grunts from him and a distracted sentence here and there.

Speaking of distance, how long had it really been since we'd had sex? My calculation of two months could have been way shorter than reality. The last time I remember, it had been hurriedly over, early in the morning before Nick had to be at work. Did he not find me attractive anymore? And more to the point, did I not find him sexually attractive? We were into such a routine, I hadn't sat down and thought about it too much until today.

Ugh. My dry spell had escalated into a full-blown drought.

Pouring some body wash onto a sponge, I slowly rubbed it over my skin, noticing when I got to my breasts that they began bristling, as if they'd been eavesdropping on my mind chatter and were giving me a huge hint. *Hello, we're still here and we're not just for decoration!*

I couldn't bring myself to become aroused thinking of Nick. The on switch to my libido wasn't connected to his name anymore, so I tried something.

Harley the hottie. Yep, that sent a zing of heat to my needy little pellets, and a rush of hormones directly south. Surely, I needed some intense therapy. Who grazed their peaks while fantasizing about a coma patient at work? Someone desperate and needy, that's who. Me. At least I wouldn't have far to walk should I need a straight- jacket. ICU to the psyche ward was only about four minutes by foot.

My body wasn't listening to logic, though. It had its own agenda, and that involved immediate release.

Turning head on into the spray, I took a few deep breaths and dropped the sponge. As much as I needed the big O, I wasn't going to allow myself to have one with my boyfriend in the other room and my mind conjuring up vivid images of a ripped, unconscious stranger.

I would go to bed frustrated as punishment for even contemplating the idea. Shame on me.

Switching the faucets off, I dried myself thoroughly and dressed in my sleeping clothes. In the bedroom, Nick hadn't moved, so I poured myself a glass of wine and threw the frozen chicken casserole into the microwave to thaw.

While I waited, my mind kept switching gears

backwards and forwards to Harley. Picking up my laptop off the coffee table, knowing full well that doing a missing person search of our town would result in nothing, but my fingers were moving over the keys before I could rationalize the stupidity of it.

I had nothing to go on. I keyed in Ann Arbor, male. Guessing his age, I'd say approximately 26–30 years old. A couple of hits came up, but weren't connected. Both were teens from last year who had been on the news channels and in the papers. Turns out the teens had run away and were found six months later in Missouri.

Damn. Dead end. I knew the search would be futile. The police would have already tried but something in me needed to find out how he had landed in my ICU room.

If the police had fingerprinted him, maybe they could get a hit, but only if he were already in the system. And being a criminal already in the system would mean we would have already had several visits by the police. They'd turned up on the scene and then the next day, from what Debbie had told me, but apart from that, we'd heard nothing.

"Hey. What are you doing? Is dinner ready?"

I startled, not expecting Nick to appear.

Closing my laptop, I rose and walked over to him, giving him a peck on the cheek. Very amicable and friendly, but nothing romantic. I should have been feeling more. I wanted to. Had we fallen so far into a rut that the spark had totally fizzled out? It would appear so. Nothing stirred in my belly. No flutter of nerves. No anticipation of great conversation and even greater sex later. Just nothing. I was officially frigid.

Pulling back, he watched me in a way I hadn't seen since we first began dating. Perhaps my obvious lack of affection had finally given him cause for concern. Had a light bulb gone off in his brain? Doubtful. Suspicion had me silently asking all sorts of questions.

His eyes held mine for a beat before I had to look away. The sudden weirdness had me confused. If he thought he could simply show a shred of interest after all this time and I'd be all over him, he was mistaken. I didn't operate like that. Resentment had formed a thin layer over my affections toward my boyfriend and he would need a chisel to make a crack.

"I'll put it on to heat. It's only just thawed out. Do you want a glass of wine?" Pulling away had me breathing easier.

"Sure." Handing him my full one, I grabbed another for myself. I moved to the microwave, noting it was about finished defrosting.

I didn't hear him approach and nearly dropped my glass when I felt his arms slip around my waist and his nose nuzzle into my neck. Okay, what? Nick hadn't instigated any form of affection for eons. Had he some strange connection to the thoughts I'd been having seconds ago? And should I be worried or happy? It was unusual for him to even make an appearance in the kitchen. How should I react? Nothing in me came to life. I was a statue.

"Mmm. You smell nice," he crooned. "Freshly showered."

My frozen libido for Nick didn't bat her pretty

eyes, but guilt bossed me around. It shouldn't have, considering how little he ever paid attention to me, but it did. My nurturing nature and need to please won out. I gave without receiving. It's how I rolled. Did I need to put more effort in? Probably. Did I want to? I wasn't sure, but didn't I owe the relationship one last chance before I bowed out? To know I had given my all. I shouldn't dismiss it totally if Nick was going to begin trying. That's what this was, surely. His attempt at trying. Shit. A thought slammed into me. Could he be having an affair? I'd heard of husbands suddenly being extra attentive when they were seeing someone else. They overcompensated at home so as not to raise suspicion.

I questioned it. Nick having an affair? Nah. I laughed silently. When would he have the time?

Leaning over to the island, I put my glass down before it fell to the floor and then I leaned back into my barely there boyfriend, attempting to feel something other than friendship.

Wondering if I should say anything, my mouth opened before I could stop it. "What's up? This is unlike you. I don't mean anything bad by it, but it's just…well, we don't do this anymore."

He tensed beneath me but didn't let go, resting his chin on my head. "I'm sorry. I've been so tied up at work lately. They're pushing me to do overtime, which is what I brought home with me. It's what I stay back for most nights." He sighed. "I miss you. I miss us."

Turning in his arms, I looked up at him. The virtual stranger. His six foot stature towered over my five six. He was handsome in his own right. Sandy straight hair, perfectly brushed into a bankers comb-over. Adequate mouth with dappled freckles on both cheeks. Boyish quality to his face. His light blue eyes peered back at me with a mixture of regret and my own mirrored guilt.

"We don't do anything or go anywhere as a couple. I feel like we're merely roomies." Hearing it out loud drove home how bad things were.

The microwave beeped, signaling dinner. It broke whatever rare moment we were having.

"Let me make it up to you. You on early shift tomorrow?" he asked.

"Yeah. Finish at five. Why?"

"Let's eat out. Dinner at seven. Gandy Dancer restaurant? I know you love seafood."

My mood elevated at the thought of eating out for a change. "Really?"

Was he really prepared to make the effort? After all this time? Maybe I underestimated him and he truly was snowed under with work and feeling guilty for not spending enough time with me. Benefit of the doubt and all that, right? If we began spending more time together, our feelings for each other would surely return to what they had been. Wouldn't they?

"Of course. Like you said, we don't do it anymore. It's time we started," I conceded.

I wasn't sure what had overcome Nick, but I found myself accepting. "That sounds lovely. I'll meet you there?"

"Yeah. I'll go straight from the office. You can finish and come home and change. That way I can still put in a little overtime and serve you at the same time."

Could we climb back up to where we were when we began dating? Things had been good for the first little while, and without either of us knowing it, life had wedged between us. A wide chasm didn't mean a bridge couldn't be constructed. As long as we began building from each side we could meet in the middle. I had felt love for him once. Could I find it buried beneath all the disappointment and frustration? Part of me wanted to believe. The other part already knew the truth.

I grabbed two plates and loaded up our dishes with the chicken casserole, moving my glass of wine over to my seat at the table. For tonight anyway, we were a normal couple. At the very least we were eating in the same room.

Chapter Five

Harley

Where had Mac gone? For hours, it felt like I was alone. No voices sang or spoke. On occasion a shuffling sound had me imagining a person nearby. Karen or someone different? I drifted on a cloud of obscurity, the laconic beep my only friend.

I needed to see something other than darkness. With my eyes fused shut, it seemed impossible. I didn't want to be in the void anymore. I had to find out what had happened to me. Whoever *me* was.

Awareness flickered like a lone flame in a draft. The battle to remain conscious tested me, especially with little inspiration to remain that way. A huge block of time passed. At least, it felt like it. I couldn't be sure...about anything. All I had were my thoughts. Nothing more. The rest of me ceased to exist as I floated again. Light and buoyant. The density gone. No body. No sensation. Eerie and yet all-consuming. An element of fear curtained my sentience. Would I be stuck here forever now? I likened it to drifting in the eternity of space with no destination.

Then something happened. An intense pull. A vacuum dragging me on a precise path. Like before, I fell, only this time, faint sounds swirled around me. The faster I plunged, the louder the noise grew until unmistakably, I recognized it as talking again. A familiar quality. I honed in all my senses to the joyous sound. My insides sparked as if a match had struck flint. The distinctive voice of my angel had returned.

Jerking to a stop didn't bother me. Or the weight pressing in from all angles. All I could focus on was her.

"Mac. Tell me about your evening." It wasn't Karen. Another stranger.

"Actually, it was better than I anticipated. Nick and I had dinner together and talked. We have both been so busy, we've been neglecting each other. He's even offered to take me to dinner tonight."

Nick? Why did the mention of his name make me a tight coil of irritation? Did she have a boyfriend? Husband? If her looks were anything like her voice, it would be a miracle if she were single. Did the guy appreciate what he had? Did he cherish her and shower her with affection? Give her flowers and take her dancing? Perhaps he did. A selfish part of me wished him to be an asshole. If she were mine, I would offer her the world.

"Oooh. Do you think he's going to propose? And the bigger question is…will you say yes?"

What? No! You can't! He can't! Wait. That means she's not married. Yet.

Even so, she'd be taken forever. The idea disturbed me way more than it should. I didn't know Mac. She didn't know me. We were strangers. So why did I hate the notion of her belonging to another?

"He's not proposing. He's married to his job. I think it's a guilt date."

That's more like it. Nick did sound like a dick. Too busy for an angel like Mac. An outright douche. Undeserving of her. Happiness broke into my anxious thoughts.

"Honey, take whatever you can get. Order the most expensive dish on the menu and bleed him dry."

Laughter. The kind that made my knees want to shudder and my insides go all gooey. I'd missed the sound. Her sound. The more of her I heard, the more I craved. She was enlivening me again. Bringing me back from the dead.

"I just…never mind."

"Oh no. Not never mind. Spill it. You've started it and you need to finish it. You just what?"

"Is it wrong to feel like we're only friends? For the first time in months, he pulled me into him last night. An intimate gesture, and well…I didn't feel anything. He's a great guy and all. A workaholic, but that aside, he's decent. I'm not sure what it is, and maybe I'm expecting too much but, I don't think he's enough anymore, you know? I want things to work, but at the same time, I don't."

"Ah ha. I do know. Trust me. He's not floating your boat. That's why my ex and I broke up. It was mutual. We both knew it wasn't going anywhere and we moved on. We're happier apart."

Silence. I could almost hear Mac thinking. If I could move my mouth, I would be grinning like a fool. Being cited as unconscious and unhearing had its perks. It allowed me to be an audio voyeur.

"I think for me, it's the whole moving out and starting on my own thing. I'm not needy, but I'm not sure I want to live alone."

"Mac, you practically live alone all the time now. If Nick's not working at the office, he's working at home." A noise like a cupboard opened and closed.

"At least if he's on his computer at the apartment, I know he's there." A loud sigh saddened me.

"Then why don't you move and advertise for a roommate?"

"Seriously? I don't think I could be bothered meeting and questioning a group of strangers, hoping I picked the right one."

"Well, you have to do something, because if you remain where you are, you'll stagnate."

"I know you're right. I think I've already done that."

"Speaking of stagnating, I'm out of here. After twelve hours of staring at Mr. Orgasm here, I'm beat."

The room filled up with Mac's laughter again…it was a sound I could listen to forever. If I remained in my black coffin and only had that one thing, it would be enough to keep me going.

Hearing one nurse leave, I knew I had Mac all to myself.

"Did you miss me, Harley? Let's have a look at you and see if there's any change."

Damn straight I missed her. Like crazy. She may never know how much. Her nearness jolted through me without even a touch. I soaked in the sensation, already happier to have her all to myself. More than anything, I longed to hear her sing, but there was no way to communicate, so hope was all I had.

The gentlest of touches sent my head into a tailspin. Featherlike and warm. My wrist was lifted and delicate fingers were clasped firmly around it. God. Her skin felt like the most expensive mink. I could have bathed in it. Encased myself in it. A scent of apple blossom had me wanting to bury my face into her and inhale the life-giving aroma into my cells. Another figment of my imagination? If I could smell, why couldn't I move or wake up?

"Pulse is normal. That's great. We need to get you better so we can find out who you are."

I don't care who I am. I only care about seeing you. Having you caress me some more.

"It's strange. Even though you probably can't hear me or understand what I'm saying, I'm happy to be at work this morning. Glad you're still here. That's not to say I don't want you to recover, because I do, more than anything…but just having you lying here is…comforting."

More. Tell me more. Don't stop talking, Angel.

I cursed the loss of her touch, which anchored me to some form of reality.

"So, anyway, I'm a little nervous about my dinner tonight. I shouldn't be, because I've been seeing the guy for two years. You'd think I'd be excited, right?"

Go on...

The silken fingers touched my forehead, causing the beeping to rocket. Panic sounded from Mac's voice.

"Shit."

Feet shuffled.

"Doctor!"

More scuffling as the apple blossom filled my senses again. "Are you waking? Can you hear me? Harley?"

The gentle mink brushed up and down my arm soothingly. If I could damn well move, I'd latch onto her. My lifeline.

Footsteps. Hurried. A door pushing open. "What is it, Nurse?"

"The patient's heart rate hit the roof. It's still elevated. One sixty beats per minute."

A masculine smell engulfed me. Cologne or aftershave with notes of sanitizing solution. How did I even know what these smells were akin to with no memory? Maybe certain things—smells and sounds—were forever ingrained into us.

"Could be a sign he's waking. It is a normal function of a coma patient to react to certain things and bring on an increase in heartrate. Take some bloods and run them through the lab. We'll see if there's any change there."

"Thanks, Doctor."

Coma? How? Why? Clearly I wasn't dead in heaven. More like a hospital on Earth. Sounds and smells carried a familiarity about them. I'd heard them before, but I couldn't place where.

"It's time to take some blood, handsome, and then I need to change your fluids and check your wound."

She called me handsome? Did she say things like that to all her male patients? Still, the primal segment of my psyche was high-fiving her moniker. I hadn't wondered about my appearance, but now that the seed had been planted, I couldn't help but try to form an image in my mind. Being immobile, I was unable to lift my hand to map out my face.

And should she be touching me so often? There were no complaints on my behalf. No. Just a blind observation. If anything, I never wanted her to let me go. I craved more of it.

Further sensation began flowing into me as I felt a pushing and pulling on the back of my hand, amidst a slight sting. Definitely on Earth.

"How about we prop you up a bit? You've been flat on your back too much. It's time to sit up. I think a sponge bath is in order too, followed by some leg and arm rotations to get the blood flowing to your extremities. We can't have that hulk of a body wasting away on us, can we?"

Ha! She'd noticed me, all right. Regardless of whether she had a boyfriend, she was a female with eyes. It pleased me to no end that I was attractive to her, even though I had no clue as to what I looked like. Or Mac, for that matter. All I had was a pretend image in my mind of a golden-haired beauty with soft skin and kind blue eyes. Her voice had crafted the image lying behind my closed eyes. If or when I could see again, I wondered how accurate the picture in my mind would be.

My body began rising into a more upright position, settling me at a sufficient angle, and then her hands were on me again, much to my delight.

"I'm going to need to unhook your gown and pull it down to access your wound, so just bear with me while I put my arms around you."

Yep. That's it. Do what you will. No complaints here. She crowded closer, raising me slightly off the bed while untying the knot at the back of my gown. I imagined if my eyes opened, I'd be flush with her breasts. Wouldn't that be an awesome sight to wake up to? Apparently my mind still remembered what the female anatomy was. Go figure.

Cool air washed over my torso.

"There. Now let's get this bandage off and changed."

Take it all off. Strip me bare. I'm at your mercy.

Would she be horrified to know my thoughts? Or would the part of her who needed something more from a man secretly cheer in glee? Not knowing myself as a man didn't matter. I would adore this woman who had brought me back from the precipice of death. She deserved to be cherished.

A small gasp had me wondering what she saw. Something gruesome? What lay under the bandage? A wound of some sort? Perhaps it had left me disfigured. Surely a nurse had seen the worst kinds of deformities. I couldn't imagine my injury being too bad.

Her velveteen touch returned, along with more pulling. I was fully present and not so much dangling in the unknown now. Each brush of her skin on mine elicited an internal shiver of the best kind.

"The surgeon did a wonderful job. This should heal up like new. You were lucky to have one of the best reconstructive specialists in the state."

Yeah, yeah. Just keep touching me. That's all I care about at this point. Contact with another. I'm lonely and I don't like the feeling. That's it, Angel. Keep your hands on my chest.

"I sure wish you could talk and tell me what happened. Are you in danger? Are you the good or bad guy? Why would someone want to shoot you?"

Wait! Shoot, you say? I've been shot? What the hell!

A chill ravaged me. Her question repeated itself in my head. Why, or more to the point, who would want to shoot me? Things like this didn't happen to normal people, did they? Did that mean I wasn't normal? Just who in the hell had I become? A pimp? A drug lord?

I can't remember. Not anything. It's like I've only just been born, and my life prior to hearing your voice doesn't exist. You're my only attachment to the world. A world I know nothing of. Without a memory I may as well have been transported to another planet.

She began stroking me as she spoke. "I know one thing. Whoever you are, you take care of yourself. These muscles don't just happen. This takes hours of work in a gym every day. Someone who looks as good as you must have someone. Girlfriend. Wife. Female friends."

My brain was tired and overworked from attempting to conjure up answers to her questions and assumptions. With her hands still resting on me, I comfortably drifted off, safe in the knowledge that she was by my side. The rest of it would have to wait. This time I welcomed the darkness.

Chapter Six

Mac

Shame is what I should have felt. *Should* being the operative word. I loved touching the smooth, taut chest of my patient without his knowledge. If anyone chose to walk in at *said moment* they would see me checking his wound. Nurse duties. To me it was an indulgence. I couldn't help my wandering hands with the feel of Harley's ripped chest beckoning me.

The temptation was too great. The man at my disposal fit the bill for the perfect specimen. His hairless torso felt warm and smooth. I imagined drizzling dark, melted chocolate over his pecs and down onto his eight pack, the brown, sweet treat getting stuck beneath the grooves, pooling in the hollows. Sweet heaven. I was in my four-walled room of sin. My lewd thoughts took hold and gripped me firmly.

My breathing became stunted by my scandalous ministrations, nurses and doctors scurrying around beyond the thick white door. Wasn't touch also good for coma patients? To let them know people were with them? To comfort?

He had no one except me and the relief nurses. If any of his senses were still functioning, wouldn't this be considered therapy?

"You're going to get me in all sorts of trouble, you know that, don't you? How can someone who looks the way you do, end up shot in an alley with no identification? It doesn't make sense." Standing, I moved to the cabinet on the far wall to grab some gauze and tape to redress the stitched hole.

Before I could return to the bed, my cell vibrated in my pocket. It didn't often ring in the day, so I pulled it out and checked the screen. Nick. Hmm. That's odd. He knew better than to call me at work.

"Hey Nick."

"Hi honey. Listen, I hate to do this to you, but we're going to have to take a rain check on our dinner tonight. I'm so sorry. An important client is in town and they're only here for twenty-four hours, so I have to meet with them, but I promise I'll make it up to you."

And there it went. The one night we had planned to go out to dinner had vanished into thin air. It seemed that we weren't meant to be together. Not while Nick worked as if his life depended on it. I'd had enough. Spending another night in the apartment alone was almost like a prison sentence. My patience had worn very thin. I should have known better than to hope we could recapture feelings of old.

"You're kidding, right? I can't believe that the

one night we actually plan, you have to cancel." Gazing at Harley, my stomach twisted in knots as I released a long, resigned sigh.

"The client has only just called me. It's very last minute. I know you're disappointed. I am too. Why don't you call one of your friends and she can take my place?"

A friend? All my friends worked at the hospital. If they weren't toiling odd hours, they were sleeping or enjoying time with their own spouses and partners who actually wanted to spend time with them.

"Fine. Whatever. I'll see you when I see you."

"Mac…"

I disconnected before he could finish. Disappointment wasn't what I was feeling. Anger and frustration were high on the list. Nothing would ever change. If I allowed myself to stay with Nick, I would keep getting the same thing. Nothing.

Switching my cell off and returning it to my pocket, I stalked over to Harley in a huff.

"Jesus Christ! I can't believe him! One night out. That's all! Is it so much to ask? A client breezes into town, expecting Nick to drop whatever he had planned, to discuss investments? Gah! Who do these clients think they are? People do have lives. And Nick, being the dedicated workaholic he is, couldn't refuse. I'll always be second on his list of priorities."

Babbling to Harley, I didn't care if he could hear me or not as I unwrapped the gauze and placed it softly over his wound before adhering it with tape.

Even if my feelings for Nick were borderline

friendship, it still annoyed me to be stood up so many times. No one else would put up with living the way I had. Why should I?

"I bet you wouldn't treat your girl like that, would you?" Watching his face for any sign of change, admiring his sooty, thick lashes fanned out, I couldn't help but balk at my life. What else did I have, apart from my job?

With both parents off traveling the world while my father took his four weeks acquired annual leave from his job as an industrial machinery engineer and no siblings, I had no one. Mom and Dad weren't due back for another three weeks and lived on the other side of town. They thought the sun shone out of Nick's butt. Being an investment banker and all, they saw him as a good provider. That may be so, but if he couldn't offer me any emotional connection or love on a regular basis, the relationship couldn't survive too much longer.

My friend-time consisted of lunch breaks at work with whoever occupied the staff cafeteria. My boyfriend time…non-existent. I'd been secretly admiring and touching a man I would never be able to have because he might not even wake up and could still turn out to be a criminal, pimp, or drug lord.

"Looks like it's going to be a long day. I'm not supposed to leave you alone, but I need a coffee. I'll be right back. After that call from Nick, a large mug with three sugars should give me the kick I need."

Checking the heart monitor, I made to leave, but only got to the door when the beeping increased to a noticeable speed once more. I paused mid-stride and swung around, my eyes fixating on the EKG machine.

Instinct had me grabbing my stethoscope and dashing to the bed, checking wires, etcetera, and then Harley's heartbeat, which sprinted. Shit.

I pressed my fingers into his carotid artery, noticing how faint it felt due to its speed. Tachycardia for the second time. All ready to page the doctor again, I jumped back and sucked in a harsh breath. Harley's eyes opened.

Chapter Seven

Mac

Two arresting peepers blearily held my own. I could see his mouth move as he attempted to speak.

Bending down, with my ear facing him, I barely heard a scratchy whispered, "Don't leave me."

I tried to remain professional, but my brain asked all kinds of silent questions. One being, how had he known I'd been about to step out? He must have heard me. That would mean he'd listened to me babble on about Nick. Just how long had he been conscious?

My body reacted to his breath on the side of my face by shivering. Pulling back, I made the mistake of finding his alluring, dark eyes. God. Now that I could see his eyes, it upped his hotness to a whole new level. For a long, drawn out moment, I took pause in their beautiful depths, enchanted with how they bedazzled me. I finally had the whole package presented to me and he took my breath away. His eyes brought him to life, as if he'd merely been a lump of flesh and bone before. For the first time in months, I became animated too. It was hard to describe how my insides rejoiced. My heart thundered. My stomach somersaulted and adrenalin ran a steady stream through my veins.

A loud clang outside brought me back to my senses, realizing I'd been *fangirling* like a teenager.

"Hi." I settled myself and morphed into nurse mode, all the while unable to sway my eyes from his charcoal ones. "You're awake. That's awesome! I'll be able to let the doctors know. You had us worried for a while, but it would appear you are going to be okay."

His mouth remained closed, he merely blinked at me.

"Would you like a drink of water? You must be thirsty."

Not waiting on his response, I grabbed the pitcher of water I'd brought in for myself and poured a small amount into a paper cup.

"Just small sips only."

Oh Mama! My hands were shuddering. Since when had another person caused me to shake so much?

Praying I could keep the water from spilling, I raised the bedhead a little more and then draped myself over him, keeping my eyes on his mouth and not his continued scrutiny of me.

"Open up." Placing the cup to his mouth, I tipped it up until the clear liquid touched his dry lips. I'd never wanted to be that paper cup more in my life. Even though his lips were dry, they looked soft. Kissable. I watched in fascination as they molded to the rim of the cup. His throat bobbed as he swallowed, causing me to do the same. They had me thinking all kinds of thoughts.

Get a grip, girl. He's a patient. You're working here. You're a professional.

Noticing him attempting to chug it down, I drew the cup away and placed it on the metal drawers beside him. "That's enough for now. Small and often is best." Pressing the pager on my hip, I hoped Chase would hurry up. Now that Harley wasn't just a lump on a bed but an awake Adonis, I stressed. What if he felt me touching him inappropriately earlier?

If he reported it to Admin, I could lose my job, and being the only stability in my life, I couldn't afford for that to happen.

As I brought my arm back down toward my side, I nearly lost it again when I felt his touch. My neck pivoted to the large, veined hand gripping my wrist.

"Mac."

Holy hell. He knew my name. He had heard stuff. Crap.

"How…I mean…did you…?" God, what a bumbling idiot.

"Angel."

"Angel?" He had my full attention now. His dark lower lashes made him look like he wore eye-liner. Combined with his mesmerizing, *sexier than thou* eyes, the room closed in. Where was Chase? My breathing stalled, his fingers pressing on my pulse point. When his eyebrow quirked slightly, it became evident he knew how he affected me.

I had to get it together, instead of floundering.

Quickly snatching my arm back, his firm grip fell away. I rotated to the door, willing someone to open it and walk through, keeping my back to him while I breathed through my reaction to his voice and his words.

Whether his scratchy tone was from being parched, I couldn't tell. Perhaps it always sounded gritty. His plea not to leave him had caught me off guard. Why had he said that? Was he scared? I guess I owed him a little understanding, given his circumstances. Waking up in a strange place with someone you didn't know must be daunting. How would I react? Probably the same.

Deciding to grow a pair, I faced him again. "You're safe. You're in the hospital in Ann Arbor. You were brought in a week ago with no identification, so we don't know who you are, where you live, or anything about you. For now, your name is Harley."

His puzzled expression failed to surprise me as I moved around the room. With the heart monitor under control, I unwrapped a syringe and inserted it into his cannula to draw some blood. I could feel his watchful eyes on me. Then again, he had no one else to stare at in the room. He probably had lots of questions running through his head.

With no prompting from me, he grated out, "Sing."

Luckily I had just taken the needle out, otherwise I may have caused him an injury with my astonishment. What on earth? His strange request had me glaring at him—through him in an attempt to figure out why he said that one word. I'd sung yesterday while working but…surely not. Had he been conscious since then? My brain kicked into high gear.

"You heard me sing? How? Did you catch everything I said?" I needed to know. None of my other coma patients had ever admitted to hearing anything, so I asked with great interest.

"Angel."

Again with the *angel* thing. Using my sleuthing skills, which came in handy being a nurse, attempting to figure out patient's symptoms among other things, I thought hard. Why would someone who had just met me call me *angel* and then ask me to sing?

The penny dropped. My voice. While pulling out of the coma, he must have mistaken me for an angel. Had he wondered if death had stolen him?

Smiling for the first time, I replied, "Well, if you say so, but I'm really not that good. I wouldn't call my voice angelic, but I do like to sing. I can't believe you heard me." Perching against the edge of the bed, I found his attention still trained on me.

"I'm glad you found some comfort in it. I've heard doctors discussing the very real notion that while in a coma, patients have some faculties. It's obviously true. Amazing really, when you think about it."

He blinked heavily.

Pondering on what song to sing, I chose, Kelly Clarkson's "Since U Been Gone."

I didn't want to appear to be singing directly to him, so I moved to tidy up the back counter, throwing away any rubbish and straightening paperwork. I absorbed myself into the lyrics, working on autopilot, as if I didn't have a one man audience who oozed intensity, hanging on every word. Singing took me to a different place, one where I was free. Nothing else mattered as I became the words, feeling the story behind the song.

When the song ended, my neck heated as I hesitantly turned in Harley's direction. He lay deathly still, and for a moment I thought he may have dozed off, but when I connected with his absurd eyes, his pupils had glassed over and his eyebrows were pressed together with emotion. He'd been moved by it.

Nick didn't care about my voice. Having someone truly connect with the lyrics the way Harley had gave me a brilliant rush. The nurses who heard me were always commenting, but nothing like this. Harley didn't have to speak. His expression told the story. Any singer would tell you the same thing. It's the connection to listeners that matter. The ability to draw them away from the tune and into the story behind the words. I'd done that and it felt amazing.

Pressing my embarrassment aside, I returned to nurse mode, needing to disconnect from his pull.

"Are you tired? You should rest. I need to go and see what's keeping the doctor and run these bloods to the lab."

I patted his hand. He swiftly turned his over so that he effectively held mine. He squeezed, taking me off guard. I needed to remember the patient/nurse rules, even though I'd already broken them.

His palm felt surprisingly warm, considering the room was cool. Mine felt tiny, almost childlike and yet, because of that the sensation, brought me comfort. Like if I held on tight, he'd protect me and never let anything happen to me.

"Stay."

That one word did things to me it shouldn't. My neglected heart opened its doors. Someone wanted me. Needed me. A foreign sensation. Sure, patients relied on nurses all the time to bring them things and take their pain away, but I always disconnected from it. I couldn't with Harley. His eyes held fright. His tone carried fear. He latched on to me as a child would, after waking from a deep sleep, crying out for their mother. Someone comforting.

"I'm not going far, I promise. Just outside the door." I went to tug my hand away, but he held firm. I glanced down as soon as I felt a shudder. His hand was quivering.

"Stay!" It was more of an order now than a plea, and I wasn't quite sure how to react. He seemed afraid to be left alone even for a moment.

"Okay. I'm not going anywhere, but I am going to have to leave this room at some stage to pee and take a break. The blood needs to be tested too."

Pressing the pager again, I could only remain at his bedside until Chase eventually showed up. He must have had an emergency to tend to. Damn, I desperately needed a coffee. Until then, I'd have to sit tight and hold Harley's hand. I guess I could handle it. Just doing my job, right?

Chapter Eight

Harley

Now that I had my bearings, and knew without a doubt I wasn't dead, and the voice I'd been hearing in my comatose state had been Mac's, I couldn't take my eyes off her.

It wasn't her shapely figure or short, blonde choppy bob haircut. It wasn't even her delicate, ivory skin I'd felt touch me more than a nurse should. No. She lit up the room with her presence, giving off some sort of magic, because I sure as hell had been ensnared in her spell. Even her leaf green eyes, which darted back and forth between mine and everything else in the room, although glorious, weren't what made her special.

I wanted to know her. Everything. What her favorite foods were. Movies. Colors. Habits.

I could tell I made her nervous by the way she swallowed thickly and tried to quell her trembling hands. Did I frighten her? I doubted that. How could I, being incapacitated? If I had to guess, I'd say she felt things that were taboo for any nurse. Her body language spoke volumes. I affected her the way she affected me.

I didn't have time to ponder it long before the door burst open and a doctor hurried in. "Nurse? You paged me? Sorry, I got tied up with Mrs. Sullivan down in room six. She had another episode."

The doctor didn't wait for Mac's reply, but found my gaze, and raised his eyebrows in surprise. "You're awake! That's great."

"That's not why I paged you, Doctor. He had another bout of tachycardia, but everything has settled down now he's awake."

The man moved over to me and proceeded to check me over as Mac had already done. Procedure, I guessed.

"I have some bloods here that need to go to the lab. Do you think I could run them down and grab a coffee while I'm out?"

My head pivoted toward her as she made her way to the door. Panic nestled low in my belly. It caused me to cry out again. "No!"

My arm came up of its own accord, palm facing the roof, fingers pointing toward her in a 'don't leave me' fashion.

Confusion mapped her face and then her mouth settled into a dazzling smile. "It's okay, Harley. I'll only be a few minutes. Doctor will stay with you until I get back. Right, Doc?"

"Yeah. You go. Who's doing breaks this morning?"

"I'm not sure, but I'll forfeit mine if I have to, as

long as I can grab a coffee."

She glanced at me again and nodded, attempting to console me. My throat narrowed to the diameter of a straw.

She must have seen the change. "You'll be fine. You need to calm down and breathe deeply and evenly."

Why did I feel like I couldn't function without her nearby?

"PTSD," the doctor said, standing beside my bed. "It's common after a traumatic experience. You were shot. It's a lot for the body and mind to cope with."

I heard him but didn't really register his words as I watched Mac quietly leave me. My jaw became rigid, teeth clenched as I attempted to suck in air. Without her, the fear closed in. Helpless. Frightened. Anxiety rose sharp and fast.

"Please," I whispered. "I need her in here with me."

Nodding, the doctor said, "It's normal under your circumstances to latch on to the person you first woke to. Mac has a way with patients which makes them feel at ease."

All I wanted to do was claw at my neck to get some air. The sterile smell of the room became too much. I wanted my angel's scent.

"Can you remember anything prior to being in hospital? Like what happened to you? We know you were shot, but apart from that we have nothing to go on."

I couldn't focus on anything except Mac. How long had she been gone? Seconds? Minutes?

Shaking my head, I squeezed my eyes shut, willing my fear to ease. I didn't like feeling this way. Desperate and needy. My brain seemed to be in control of my body, and normally that might be a good thing, but not in this case.

"Where is she?" I grated out, eyes still sealed tightly. I didn't care if I sounded crazy. Nothing mattered except Mac's return. Now.

A chuckle had me open them to see the amused doctor.

"It's only been three minutes. How will you cope when she leaves for the day?"

The thought hadn't crossed my mind. I'd already spent nights without her before gaining full-consciousness. But being able to see her made her real. And being real had my need for her at an all-time high. It didn't make sense, but at this point, nothing did.

"We can give you something to help you sleep to keep you comfortable. How's your pain level now? Do you need any meds?"

Focusing on my body, I could feel a tightness in my chest where my wound sat. It wasn't pain exactly. More like discomfort. "Not yet."

I didn't like the idea of sleep either. Being back in the nothing. Alone. My lids were leaden, and if not for my brain fighting it off, I'd fall asleep in seconds.

The doctor fussed and proceeded to read my chart while he waited, killing time. We didn't converse again. I turned my head toward the window, which looked out onto another wing of the hospital. Nothing special, but perhaps if I focused on something other than my angel's absence, it would help me calm down.

Did I normally get stressed out? Were the snippets of my nature peeking through, the real me? I hoped not, because I hated the sensation of panic and despair.

It took ages for Mac to reappear. It felt like it, anyway. Seeing her face again made me sag into the bed.

Immediately I calmed. She carried her coffee and placed it on the countertop opposite me. My whole body cheered with relief. My chest muscles relaxed and my breathing evened out.

"What took so long?" Turning to me, she failed to meet my gaze.

Glancing at her watch, her eyebrows rose. "Ah, I practically ran to the lab and then it took a couple of minutes to make the coffee. All in all, I'd say that was a world record."

"Indeed, Mac. Thanks for being so prompt. I've got a ton of patients to see." The doctor walked to the door and turned at the last minute, smiling at Mac. "I'll leave you to it then." He quickly looked at me, and then turned and left us alone.

"So, now that you are awake, we'll get the ball rolling to have you moved to a ward." She only gave me a flicker of attention while she placed some new meds into a cabinet.

What? No. That would mean losing her. I couldn't have that. Jesus. I'd only just woken up. I needed to be in ICU. Couldn't she see that? Did she want me to go?

"I'm not ready. I should stay here." It came out

as childish, but I didn't give a rat's ass.

She pulled a chair out from the corner of the room and dragged it beside the bed and sat down. Her garden aroma teased my senses.

"Well, patients don't get a choice. ICU is for critical and high care patients. You're stable now. We need the room for others coming in. I will visit you, though. I promise."

Her green eyes with flecks of yellow watched me with sympathy. It did little to quell the whirlpool of disquiet.

"You don't understand. I can't leave here. I can't leave…you." It was insane to hear the words. My brain wasn't communicating in any way, shape, or form. My mouth had its own agenda. I'd become clingy and desperate.

Her sensual lips parted, forcing me to lick mine.

"It's not my decision. You have to understand. It's hospital procedure." Her quiet voice sounded unsure. The hands in her lap, fiddled unnecessarily.

Screw hospital procedure. Time for brutal honesty. I had nothing to lose. "I'm scared. I don't know who I am or where I've come from. You make it easier to breathe. Only you do that. I don't know why. Just…please! Don't leave me! You're all I've got." She had to hear the truth. I needed to pull out all the stops to get her to understand. I was sinking in an ocean of amnesia. There was nothing I could grab onto. Except her.

Nervousness floated over her features as she bit the corner of her bottom lip. "You shouldn't put that on me. I'm your nurse. Nothing more. I can't be with you twenty-four seven. I have a life outside this place." Her eyes were cast downward. She couldn't even look at me while she spoke.

The words were whispered, as if she needed to convince herself. I'd heard her talking about her life and it didn't sound like she had much of one at home.

"Your boyfriend is an asshole." It was out before I could stop it. My brain had officially switched off. It felt liberating, all the same.

"Excuse me?" She froze after raising her head. Fire danced across her features, blended with disbelief.

"I heard what you said to me. He's married to his job. He doesn't appreciate you. You're an afterthought." Nothing like shooting straight from the hip.

Her eyes expanded further. "He's trying. His job is stressful and takes up a lot of his time but he's doing it for us." I didn't believe her for a second. And neither did she.

I balked. "You can't seriously buy that. Any guy would be crazy not to treat you like a queen. If you were my girl…"

She cut me off, raising a hand. "Stop! Don't say things like that. I'm not your girl. Please, we can't be talking about this." Amongst the sting of her words, I noticed sadness in her eyes. Her shoulders fell that little bit further and her mouth pressed firmly in resignation.

I knew I'd crossed the line, but damn it, the longer she spent in the room with me, the more she burrowed under my skin. The fact that her partner, a guy who should adore her, put his work above his girl, bothered me immensely.

"I just don't want to lose you as my nurse." If I got put into a regular ward, I'd never see her, despite her promise to visit. It's not like she could frequently leave her post in ICU. She'd have another patient to take my place.

Her features softened as she sat forward. "Look. I don't mean to sound so harsh. I appreciate the fact that you like the way I've been caring for you and want it to continue. You wouldn't be the first one to get attached to their nurse. It happens all the time. Trust that you will be fine without me."

She didn't get it, and I didn't really, either. I couldn't explain what I felt when she wasn't near. I just knew I didn't like it. In her presence, I had an identity. Harley. Without her I became John Doe again. A no one. God, did I have money in the bank? If I had plenty of the green stuff, I'd pay her to be my personal nurse.

How could I even find out my real name? Did I have a home somewhere? A car? A job? Surely someone would be able to identify me, otherwise on record, I would simply cease to exist. Mac had brought me back to life. That meant something. My light. My angel.

My eyes traced the curve of her hips, rising to the swell of her breasts, pausing for a moment, admiring the view before ascending to her stunning eyes.

She watched me scrutinize her and it caused my stomach to tumble.

"I'll help you find out who you are and where you're from, but you have to move to the ward when they come to collect you. It will probably be this afternoon. Now that you're awake, the nurses will get you up walking."

Did I really have a choice? I sure as hell wasn't going to like it, but if I could get up and move about, I'd be able to visit Mac, surely.

The slithering unease continued to wind itself around my insides, but I didn't protest any further. Her hands were tied by protocol. I'd just have to make the best of it. Besides, finding out where I came from topped everything else. It needed to happen before my release. Otherwise, where would I go? Stepping outside the walls of the hospital would be an alien world. Without Mac, I'd be lost.

"Fine. Thank you. I appreciate you offering to help me."

"Of course. Everybody needs a little help sometimes, right?"

Indeed. And she truly didn't know how much help I needed.

Chapter Nine

Mac

It shook my foundation when Harley admitted to needing me. His desperation made me almost cave to his wishes to have him stay in ICU by declaring a setback in his health to my peers, but my lie would catch up with me soon enough. I didn't need that kind of trouble following me.

Apparently, he couldn't remember a thing, which must be extremely alarming for him. It would serve me well to step into his shoes for a moment.

He truly had no one…except me, it would appear. My heart went out to him in sympathy. I wasn't sure how I could possibly figure things out for him when the hospital had hit a brick wall. It didn't make sense. The police who had initially come in while I was on holiday had come up blank. Was he a ghost?

Hopefully with time he would regain snippets of memory, so we could piece together his puzzle.

For now, he'd just have to get used to being in a

ward with other patients and different doctors and nurses. As much as I would miss him, at least I knew he'd be taken care of.

Perhaps I'd ask Nick if any of his friends had a spare room Harley could stay in until he got on his feet again. I didn't like the idea of him living out on the streets. My duty of care as a nurse needed to extend above and beyond in this case.

As if tuned in to my thoughts, Char came breezing through the door with two orderlies in tow pushing a bed.

"Hey girl. I'm here to steal your man." She laughed at her own joke and I couldn't help but smile at her way with words. "There's a bed free down in ward C."

Her gaze roamed over Harley. "Well, hello there. It's good to have you awake," she flirted, flashing him her killer smile.

He shot me a quick, panicked look before focusing on Char. "Are you going to be my new nurse?" The transfer had to take place regardless of his concerns.

"Nope. I'm just here to send you on your way. Chris and Jared will take care of you and see to it you get to your new room in one piece."

Harley dragged in a deep breath. Char didn't know what had transpired of late. I hadn't seen much of her, so she had no idea about Harley's attachment to me.

Moving closer to him, I said, "You ready?" Noting his apprehension and fingers squeezing the sheets, I touched his arm. "Remember what we talked about? I promise everything is going to be fine. I'll come visit you after my shift later, okay?"

His pupils had dilated in fear, and his breathing had bottomed out.

"Come on. Let's do this," I offered.

With a shake of his head, he whispered, "Please. I don't want to go."

"I know." Glancing at Char and the two orderlies, I tried to convey my concern. Char was the one who picked up on it, so she stepped in to help.

"Let's get you settled in your new room. You're sharing with a guy about your age. I'll grab you a coffee and switch the television on. You like sports, Harley?"

She realized her mistake as soon as she said it.

He appeared to think, and then went to open his mouth, but nothing came out. He couldn't remember if he liked sports or not.

Char, ever the optimist, covered her mistake. "Of course you do. You're a guy. All guys love sports." She grabbed one of his arms to help him up. Pulling back the sheets, she realized the catheter was still attached. "Oh. You want to take care of this Mac?" Her questioning gaze spoke volumes about me forgetting to do it.

"Sure." I should have done it. I normally wouldn't forget something so important but Harley threw me off my game. Pushing Harley back down, I quickly drew the curtain around the bed.

"This is going to sting a little, okay? But once it's out, you can move around and use the bathroom on your own."

Following my lead, he rested his head back on

the pillow, enabling me to lift his gown. Gingerly I removed the catheter, glancing at his face to garner his discomfort. He barely batted an eyelid, all the while he focused on me. I wondered what he thought as he watched me. His black pupils must have been magnets, because it was hard to look away. They were the most intense eyes imaginable. His stare became a living entity I could feel inside me, even with my focus elsewhere. The naughty part about being so close to him? I soaked it up and craved more. The ICU would be cold and sterile once more without him. But I had to stay strong and do my job. Nothing good would come from getting attached to a patient. They were transient.

After we were done, I pulled the curtain and nodded to Char that he was good to go.

Harley rose and swung his shaky legs over the side of the bed, sitting for a moment to stabilize.

The idea of not seeing him every day made my stomach curdle. I wasn't sure who my next patient would be, but they wouldn't have a patch on Harley.

Steadying him on the other side, I helped him shuffle to the gurney, where he climbed up, wincing as he lay down. His wound would be sore for a while.

Jared piped up for the first time. "Right. Cargo on board. Let's go deliver the freight!" He winked at me and I chuckled, keeping my sights firmly on Harley as he craned his anxious face around to watch me as they wheeled him out.

My heart broke at his pleading eyes, until the door shut behind them and I was left with Char.

"Okay, what just happened, Mac? I think pretty boy has the hots for you, and clearly he's affecting your ability to think." She leaned her hip against the vacant bed.

Letting some of the tension out on a long sigh, I folded my arms across my chest. "He's suffering from PTSD. I'm his connection. The first person he saw when he woke up. He wanted me to keep being his nurse. I explained to him the impossibility of it, given I work in ICU."

"You think he'll remember anything?"

"I hope so, because it's the only way I can help him figure things out."

She raised her eyebrows. "You're going to help him? On a personal level? What will Nick say?"

I cringed. She'd never liked Nick, so it surprised me that she asked.

"Nick quite possibly will never know. He's too busy trying to make more money. I'm convinced I could move Harley into our apartment and Nick would be none the wiser because he's never there, or if he is, it's in body only."

"You thought any more about giving him his marching orders or moving out?"

"I've been mulling it over."

"You have? So you agree with me?" She straightened, her eyes sparking with hope.

"He stood me up for dinner again."

"Ah, what a dick. Sorry, girl, but there's no excuses. Get out now and move on." Swinging around to face the door and taking a few steps before glancing over her shoulder, she added, "Who knows? Mr. Hottie, Harley could be just who you're looking for."

With that she disappeared into the bowels of the hospital before I could give her my rebuttal.

I didn't have time to dwell on it because I was paged to the nurse's station.

Chapter Ten

Mac

After a hectic afternoon, my feet were aching and I had a rotten headache. A motorbike accident victim arrived in Harley's old room after a three hour surgery. Unfortunately, the other male who'd been driving, died an hour after arriving at the hospital from internal bleeding and a brain injury.

My new guy had cheated death also, still classed as critical, but hanging in there for now. I only hoped he survived the night.

I promised Harley I'd drop by to see him, so I had to honor my vow. In actual fact, I couldn't wait to see him.

Char had been scheduled to take over my shift until midnight. She was pulling a double to get the overtime and extra money. I don't know how she did it. When she breezed through the door looking way better than me, I felt more than ready to leave. I figured she must keep herself hyped up on extra strong coffee with loads of sugar.

"Hey Mac. How's the new guy?"

"No change. Still classed as critical."

"It's going to be a long night then."

"Yep. I'm heading over to see Harley before I go."

Her eyebrows lifted, "Oh?"

"I promised him I would, being his first day in the ward."

"Uh huh."

"What's uh huh?" Her mischievous smile spoke volumes.

"I think you have an iddy-biddy crush on *his hotness*."

Turning and padding toward the door so she couldn't see through my façade, I opted for nonchalance. "He's a patient. That's all. It's my duty of care to make sure he's settled in."

"If you say so. Love you, girl."

Giving her a backward wave without spinning around, I grabbed my bag and exited, glad to be away from her accurate assumptions.

Just because I found Harley strikingly attractive didn't mean anything. The fact he had attached himself to me because of his amnesia didn't factor into it. It couldn't.

After clocking off, I followed the long hallways to ward C, my stomach tying itself in knots.

I didn't need to be nervous. I'd only seen him that morning.

I shook it off and found his room. I slowly pushed the door open, knowing he shared with another patient.

His bed lay adjacent to the large window

overlooking the hospital courtyard. Outside, the sun lowered itself for the evening, erasing some of the natural light from the room.

I could still make out Harley's rock solid form sprawled out on top of the bed sheets, his face turned toward the window. The bed closest to the door had the curtain drawn, so I couldn't see his roommate.

Careful not to disturb him, I quietly closed the distance to Harley and peeked across the bed.

His eyes were shut, his face far from restful. His forehead had a wide slash across it and his mouth cut a thin, compressed line into his cheeks.

I wondered what went on inside his head.

A sound leached from his throat. A pained grunt, as if he'd been clobbered by a plank of wood.

Moving around the bed so I faced him, I dragged a chair across and sat, praying he remained asleep. He needed all he could get in order to recover, and remembering how much he had fought against moving out of ICU, I didn't want to wake him.

It was nice to sit and take a load off. Placing my purse on the floor, I sagged into the hard chair, letting myself relax, enjoying the end of my shift. If Harley wasn't going to wake up, he wouldn't know I'd come by to visit, so I'd just have to get one of his nurses to pass on the message that I'd been.

With each minute that ticked along, Harley became more and more agitated. A thin sheen of sweat pebbled his brow, and his head thrashed from side to side.

His mumbled words were incoherent. His chest rose and fell heavily. A part of me wanted to take away his suffering, and the other part had me curious as to what caused it.

Before I could take my next breath, he cried out and sat upright in bed, eyes wide open.

I startled. The movement made him pivot his head. The alarm in his eyes denoted a man reliving a horrific memory. His pupils were dilated, his stare absent. He wasn't back yet.

I placed my hand gently on his forearm. "Harley? Hey. You had a nightmare. It's okay. It's over now."

As if remembering to breathe again, he began siphoning in air harshly, his hands coming to grip his head.

"Angel..." he said amidst panic. And then a whisper. "It wasn't a dream."

"It wasn't?"

Shaking his head, he squeezed his eyes closed, still dragging in air. "I...I. Killed. A. Friend."

Chapter Eleven

Harley–Moments before

Deathly silence. Nothing stirred. My body, swathed in weaponry, cumbersome yet necessary for battle. My mission? To seek and destroy. Take no prisoners. I had orders to kill.

My earpiece rang out. "Tigers are sitting pretty, over."

"Hold. I repeat, hold."

"Roger that."

Adrenalin powered blood in and out of my heart. I thrived on it. The lull before the storm. Everyone tense and fired up, focused solely on their target, breathing kept to silent gasps. I felt my second in command and best friend, Viper, aka Charlie O'Donnell, behind me. He'd acquired the title of Viper because of his lightning fast reflexes.

He always had my back. There were only two of us entering the front of the dilapidated building to retrieve one of our own who'd been captured by rebel militants in Afghanistan. The building was surrounded by my team, strategically placed and ready to act at my command.

Intel had led us here. A crumbling mud brick dwelling in a desert environment. The heat stifled us, all geared up, but I knew in my core, I'd been born to do this.

With an ear to the door, I listened for any activity inside, but came up empty. Motioning with my left hand to Viper, I counted down using three fingers, and then we were through the door, moving like ghosts, guns raised, eyes riveted to the thermal scopes. The interior consisted of a short hallway leading to an open space. We flattened ourselves against the wall, on high alert for the enemy. Even though we took the enemy by surprise, we still remained vigilant at all times. To let our guard down would kill us. I gave Viper the signal to stand on the opposite wall as we sidled our way to the main room, which held our target.

Nearing the space, I could see an old mattress on the floor with rumpled sheets. Red heat showed up through my scope to the left as I peeked around the corner. A partition separated part of the room. Behind it was our target. Two different distinct shapes were showing. One moving, one not.

We were like predators stalking prey. Crouched, ready to fire. Viper scoped out the rest of the room behind us as I crept forward. Our target sat, hands bound behind the chair.

The captor hovered nearby, but far enough away for me to get a clear shot without injuring our man.

Civilians would be sweating and freaking out about now, but I remained as cool as a cucumber and I knew all my men would be the same. That's what we were trained for. The elite. The best of the best. The ability to operate like a machine with no emotion attached whatsoever. We had a job to do, albeit a deadly one. We were all immersed in our roles, otherwise none of us would be here.

Clearing the rest of the house, I waited until Viper had my back, and then proceeded forward. The enemy closed the distance on our prize, negating the clear shot I'd scoped.

A voice rang out in Dari, better known as Persian. I didn't understand a word, but when the sound of a grunt followed, from our man, I acted. Rounding the corner of the partition, I barked out, "Arms up! Arms up!" He wouldn't understand, but we'd taken him off guard. A knife pressed into the prisoner's throat, the captor suddenly screaming at us. Highly agitated, he began sweating.

Viper appeared beside me, both of our guns trained on the target's forehead. Everything that ensued happened in slow motion. The bearded Afghan militant swiped his blade across Reno's throat, clean and neat. We called him Reno because he grew up in Reno, Nevada before moving to Ann Arbor two years ago, claiming he'd met a woman whom he loved. I'd never met her, because apparently she worked a lot and when she had time off, they liked to spend it together. Just the two of them. I'd asked him where they met and he'd said, online. I guess, whatever worked for some. He'd seemed happier than I'd ever seen him.

Reno had been with my team for the last two tours and I respected him as much as I did Viper.

Before I could think further, Viper and I had opened fire using our Colt M4A1 assault rifles. When the sack of shit hit the floor, my eyes flew to Reno's for the first time. His scared eyes were honed on mine, his throat slashed open, blood pulsing out from the wound and his mouth. I acted on instinct. "Cover me, Viper," I growled.

Dropping my weapon, I ran to Reno, knowing I'd failed him and knowing he knew I had. I tried to hold his throat together in a feeble attempt to redeem myself, but as his eyes began to roll back in his head and gurgles sounded out of his mouth, I let go a string of curses.

"Stay with me, buddy. We're gonna get you out of here. Stay, please!"

He was fading fast. The blood seeped through my fingers as I attempted to hold him together. The sounds coming from him weren't right. My voice was desperate. The air had soured with the coppery scent.

"Reno! Reno! Don't you do this! Don't leave me!"

His eyes opened but they were glazed with the look of death. I could see the life draining out of him.

In a final attempt to get words out, he spluttered three words that sounded very much like, "I'm sorry, man."

When his head lolled forward onto my blood-soaked hand, I let my emotions back in, guilt and anger flooding my veins.

Roaring out, I stepped back and aimed my rifle on the already dead man whose head had been blown apart and fired off numerous rounds into his chest.

Feeling a hand on my arm and a voice that wasn't Viper's, I jerked around, suddenly not in the dank room of murder and carnage but sitting vertical in a bed with a stunning woman watching me, concern marring her features.

"Harley? Hey. You had a nightmare. It's okay. It's over now."

"Angel…it wasn't a dream."

"It wasn't?"

Shaking my head as I dragged in air, I spluttered, "I…I. Killed. A. Friend."

Chapter Twelve

Harley

Her face morphed into one of complete shock. I could have been looking for things that weren't there, but I swore I noticed disappointment too.

"You're remembering your past?"

Breaking eye contact, I dragged a hand over my left cheek. "I think I know what I did for a living."

She leaned in further. "Tell me." Her sweet breath soothed my climbing heart rate.

"I was in combat. Army, military. I'm not one hundred percent sure which one. I was in a war zone. My team and I were rescuing one of our men." The memory returned full force of Reno's haunted eyes seconds before he died. A look that would forever gut me. Sucking in air, I fought for control. The memories which had surfaced were not what I'd been hoping for. I'd rather not remember anything. The dream revealed the first snippets of my past and there were emotions attached. I'd lived it.

A hand came to rest on top of mine. I searched her face for understanding or compassion and found instead, a piqued curiosity and a nod for me to continue.

"A mission I led ended badly. One of my men, Reno, died while I stood and watched." My heart squeezed tighter, catching my breath. My skin crawled with pinpricks of guilt.

Droplets fell from my eyes, a foreign sensation because of my loss of memory or my ability to be able to deaden my emotions. I'm a soldier. A killer. As much as my recollections informed me of that, the *me* who lay in a hospital bed couldn't grasp any of it. I didn't feel like a warrior. I felt like a person lost, waiting to be found. Vulnerable.

Mac dug into her purse and pulled out some tissues, handing them to me.

"I think there's more to it than that. You're being too hard on yourself. I'm sure if you could have saved him you would have done everything possible."

Her words had more tears flowing. I didn't feel like I was ever going to stop.

"I'm sorry. I feel like a weak child." The dam had burst, tapping into an unseen reservoir. The deluge hit me hard and fast. Had I been so invested in this guy Reno that his loss affected me so? Failure gripped me. I didn't know how to deal with it.

"Don't apologize. This is the start of your past coming back to you. It's great news. The rest will hopefully follow and you can get your life back."

Shaking my head, I blurted out, "I don't want my

life back. Not that one."

"It's okay. You have a choice as to what you want to do with the information you remember, but there's so much more than your job. What about family? Friends? A wife? Don't you want to know?"

Sinking back into the bed, I shut my eyes. I wanted to forget the memory. I didn't like the way it made me feel. Nausea swirled like an angry river below my breast bone. I could sense the onset of panic beginning.

"Is that all you remember? Or is there more?" Her voice pacified me.

"No. Nothing else."

Glancing down and then back up to me, she nodded and changed the subject, suddenly edgy.

"Well, I just popped in to say hi and see how you were doing. It's time for me to head home."

The thought of being without her overnight while I fought with demons from my past had me all kinds of crazy.

"Don't go! Stay and eat with me. Please? Unless of course you need to get home to your boyfriend." The mention of his name added to my sorry state. I wanted to meet the guy and see what sort of person could spend so much time working when he had a woman like Mac to go home to. If it were me…

"Harley. I can't have dinner here. Not only is the hospital food crappy, I'm tired, and really want to go home and have a bath."

She did look exhausted, but I wasn't ready to give up yet.

"Please, just a little longer. I need you to take my

mind off the memory." I reached out and touched her hand, the warmth of it taking me off guard. My eyes shot to hers, pleading.

A frown marred her otherwise perfect features, "It could have been a dream, right? How do you know for certain you lived it?"

She didn't move to pull her hand away, and the slight contact had my heart rate slowing and my breathing evening out.

"I just know. I recall the names of my team. Their faces. Voices. Every minute detail down to the smell of Reno's blood."

Sighing, she glanced at our hands before refocusing on my eyes. "I said I would help you. When I leave here, I'll start searching for your friend who was…" She swallowed heavily as if the next word lodged in her throat, "…killed. Do you know his civilian name?"

Pain lanced through me again as I remembered Reno. His last moments. What must he have been thinking and feeling? Searching my mind, I couldn't place anything else.

"I…I don't remember. I do know Viper's name, though. Charlie. Charlie O'Donnell."

"I'll start there."

"Thank you."

A staff member entered. "Mac? I didn't expect to see you here. You visiting?" Her dark eyes turned toward me.

Mac smiled at the woman, "Hey Dianne. Yes. I looked after him in ICU. Just checking up to see how he's doing."

Dianne returned her smile. "That's why you're

so popular. You genuinely care about your patients. Don't forget, you need to have a life outside of this place too."

"I know. Nick's always working though, so I figure I might as well be here doing what I do best."

Dianne shook her head on her way to the bed beside me, poking her head through the drawn curtain. "Would you like some dinner?" she asked my neighbor who I had yet to meet.

A raspy voice returned with an, "Okay. Thanks."

Male. Definitely male. He seemed content in his cocoon. I wasn't up to talking to strangers and making small talk, so it suited me fine.

Giving my roommate his food, Dianne moved to the dinner trolley and turned to Mac. "You need a permanent bed here, girl."

Mac giggled and I felt it all the way to my toes.

"You know it. It would be a hell of a lot cheaper than paying rent!"

The middle-aged woman brought my dinner to me, drawing my bedside tray across my lap and placing the dish down.

Dianne replied with a thoughtful expression, "That's not a bad idea. Free food. Free roof over your head. Hell, I may just consider it." She grinned and winked before heading out with her restaurant on wheels.

After she left, I focused on Mac, feeling a twinge of guilt over my selfishness. "I'm sorry."

Surprised, she asked, "What for?"

"Wanting you here. I've only been thinking of myself. I don't mean to keep you from your life. It's selfish of me."

As much as I wanted her to stay, I knew I couldn't expect it.

"I get it. You must be so scared. Waking up not knowing who you are, and then having a memory of life in a warzone. I can't begin to imagine what you're going through, so don't feel bad. It's my job to care about my patients. I'll stay until you finish dinner, but then I have to go. I've got to be back here at eight in the morning."

Seizing the opportunity to mention her *barely there boyfriend*, I wanted to return the offer of support. "If you want to discuss things not involving the hospital, I'm a good listener."

I hoped she could read between the lines. I'd opted for subtlety.

She stared at me a moment. Not with malice, but with a look of caution. "I…uh…I don't think that's a good idea."

"Fair enough, but the offer is there."

Turning to my food, I left the subject open. She could mull over the decision to open up to me.

Pulling the silver lid off, the plate revealed a roast dinner. My stomach cheered in the form of a loud gurgle.

Mac chuckled, the sound permeating my senses. "Your first proper meal, huh?"

"Yep. I'm starved. Can't remember the last time I ate…" Wow! The harsh truth caused my jaw to flex in frustration. Mac cleared her throat and changed the subject.

"So, you'll be allowed to leave in a few days. I'd like to offer you a place to stay until I can organize something with Nick."

Shocked at her proposal, I paused with the fork to my mouth and let my eyes pivot to hers. "Your place?" I must have been hearing things.

"Of course, I haven't asked my boyfriend yet, but I'm sure he'll be okay with it once he learns of your situation."

I wasn't so sure, but didn't want to rock the boat. "I don't want to impose."

"It's no bother, truly. And where else would you go?"

The truth? I had nowhere to go, not while I couldn't remember where I lived.

Puffing out a breath, I didn't have a choice. "As soon as I can, I'll leave, I promise. Thank you for the offer. It's very kind of you."

"It's settled then. We have a spare room. I'll get it tidied up for you."

Shoveling a heap of meat and potatoes into my mouth, I couldn't help but wonder what it would be like to live under her roof. To see her outside of the hospital. In her own environment. With her boyfriend. That thought didn't sit right in my chest. A niggle of jealousy swept over me. God. I had no right feeling anything like that. It would serve me well to set aside any blossoming emotions for Mac and focus on getting my full memory back. Distractions would only complicate things.

Chapter Thirteen

Mac

What had I done? My mouth had moved of its own accord. The idea of having Harley in my personal space wreaked havoc on my mind. He already had me feeling things I shouldn't. Inviting him into my home had been stupid and whimsical, especially considering I hadn't asked Nick. I'd been far too approving of his reaction when I'd told Harley that his moving in would be fine. Truth was, Nick would probably spit chips. I had no other choice. Tonight, if he got home at a reasonable hour, I'd broach the subject and attempt to make him see reason. I'd been going to ask him if a friend had a spare room, but somehow the idea of Harley living with someone other than myself while he recovered didn't sit well.

Keeping up my level of professionalism at the apartment would be a hard act. I would no longer be his nurse, but his housemate. Knowing his reaction to me, I'd need to be on guard and keep things strictly platonic. Friends. I could do that. Right?

His eyes had portrayed a level of sadness when I left and I'd wanted to stay just so I didn't have to witness that look in his eyes, but at the same time, I needed to get out of the damn hospital. To get some separation.

On my way home I'd veered into a Subway outlet and ordered a healthy sub for dinner. Too tired to cook, I'd made it my *go to* place sometimes after work when I knew Nick wouldn't be home.

Imagine my surprise when I found his car in the garage as I pulled up to the apartment.

So much so that I actually sat for a few minutes, pondering all the reasons why he'd come home. I figured I'd have another couple of hours on my own to soak in a tub and drown in a couple of glasses of wine before getting into a conversation about Harley.

Nervously, I parked in the garage and made my way inside.

Walking through to the kitchen, I placed my sub on the table, took a bottle of wine out of the fridge and grabbed a glass down from the cupboard. I needed a few sips to give me liquid courage. I knew he'd be in the bedroom on his laptop.

"Nick?" I called out.

Silence. Well, if he wasn't answering me, he could wait.

Popping the cork on the bottle, I poured a glass of red liquid and took a large gulp before sitting down and unwrapping my dinner. It smelled amazing. Probably because I hadn't cooked it. Chowing down, I devoured it in no time, the hole in my stomach having been filled. Tossing the wrapper in the garbage bin, I headed down the hallway.

Pushing open the bedroom door, I wasn't too far off. Nick sat on the office chair, facing his computer, talking on his cell. "Yeah…okay. I understand, but this client is an important one. It could mean huge dividends. I'm working on it…I'll stay up all night if I have to…."

Shaking my head, tamping down my disappointment, not needing to hear anymore, I shut the door, leaving him to it. Tonight I would sleep in the spare room so he could pull an all-nighter once again for his precious job. Telling him about Harley moving in would have to wait. A mammoth hot soak in the tub was my priority. I wondered if Nick even knew I'd come home.

More and more, I began to understand how bad things really were. How had I not been bothered by it before? Perhaps because Harley had given me more attention in twenty-four hours than Nick had in six months. My friends were right. I did deserve better.

Filling the tub, I stripped and climbed in, groaning as I sank deep, enjoying the effect of the hot water on my tired body. The sound also brought forth sordid images of Harley's carved chest under my fingertips. Skin pulled so tight over layers of shredded muscle, I'd had a hard time focusing on work. If his memory served him correctly and he had been a soldier in the military, it would also stand to good reason that his job demanded he be in optimal shape.

Angel. Did he really think of me as such? The

endearment sparked an unaccustomed heat inside.

Closing my eyes, I let my mind wander. Did Harley have a partner? Did they have children? The idea of him being spoken for disheartened me. It shouldn't, considering I had a boyfriend. Kind of.

What would it be like to have a man like Harley as a boyfriend? Would he be attentive? Caring? He set me off balance with his intensity. His eyes, when they drilled into me, opened me bare. He oozed masculinity. Raw with a dash of untamed. A piece of me craved more than routine and mediocre.

"Mac?"

Surprise had me snapping my eyes to the door. "Yes?"

"Don't worry about dinner for me. I'm waist deep in work. I'll grab something later."

Yep. Bingo. My life.

"Fine. I'll sleep in the other room so you can focus."

"Appreciate it."

He padded off, leaving me pissed.

Downing the remainder of the glass of wine, I rose and toweled off, strutting haughtily into the bedroom to grab my pajamas, watching the back of Nick's head the whole time, wondering if he would turn as I purposely slammed the top drawer of the dresser shut. Nope. Not even a flinch. Damn, the man! Giving him the middle finger, I flounced out after getting the sudden urge to throw his computer monitor out the window.

Eyeing my laptop on the coffee table in the living room, I made myself comfortable and began my search for Charlie O'Donnell. It was the only full name I had. Time to get started on helping Harley.

There were quite a few hits on Google with several images appearing, so I clicked on each one, hoping for a lead. Most links led back to Facebook pages and a few to websites. Investigating further for any evidence of involvement in the defense force had me hitting brick walls time and time again. Nothing. Articles told of no one in the forces by the name of Charlie O'Donnell. Hope left me. If Harley and his crew were military, all the information would be classified and under the radar.

Throwing my head back against the sofa, I took a couple of deep breaths. So much for that idea. The only other option? Wait and hope Harley got more memories back. That could take weeks. Months. Maybe never. All the while, he'd be living under my roof, tempting me with his sultry eyes and lips made for kissing.

Trouble had officially attached itself to me.

Chapter Fourteen

Mac

The next few days flew by. When I wasn't at work or visiting Harley, I scoured the internet for a hint at his true identity, coming up empty each time.

On Friday morning, I had just stepped out of the ICU, housing my now-awake motorbike accident victim who did have ID. Blake Peterson. Aged 23. Resident of Ann Arbor. He'd miraculously survived the same way Harley had.

Turning the corner to get a coffee while on my morning break, I plowed into concrete, causing me to stumble back and cuss.

"Shit," I groaned, more startled than hurt.

"Angel. Slow down."

Not expecting the familiar moniker with its sultry drawl, I squeaked out, "Harley?"

Finding his face, I almost fell back down when I witnessed a cheek smashing, teeth blinding smile that could rival the sun on a summer day.

"That's me."

He wore blue scrubs. "What are you doing?"

"They've let me out. I came to find you to let you know. I'll hang around until you finish."

"You're wearing scrubs?" Even hospital attire complimented him.

"My nurse dug these out. I don't have clothes. Apparently my shirt had to be cut off in the ambulance." He carried a bag. Seeing me eying it, he offered, "The jeans I wore when I got shot. They're…ahh…dirty."

My eyes wandered to his feet, which were now covered in black boots. They looked comical against the hospital attire, but I hid my amusement. "Right. Well, it's going to be a long day for you. I don't finish until six. I'm on my way to get a coffee. You want one?"

His eyes lit up. "Sure."

"Wait here. I'll be right back. How do you take it?"

He smirked and I felt my neck heat up with lewd thoughts. "Black. No sugar."

Coughing, unable to speak, I spun away and followed the hallway to the staff room, attempting to settle the flapping butterflies in my chest.

When I returned, he hadn't moved. He stood up straighter when he saw me, offering me a ghost of a smile.

"We can sit out in the courtyard if you wish. I'm sure you're itching for some sunshine."

"That I am."

Following me for a minute, I led him into a patient enclosure with a few tables and chairs. People were scattered around and looked up as we entered, obviously thinking Harley worked at the hospital. If only they knew.

"So…" he began, before we settled at a two-seater round table with chairs. "Did you manage to dig anything up about me?"

Disappointed I didn't have a thing, I shook my head. "No. Not yet. I'm not giving up, though. There has to be a way of finding out just who you are. Have you had any more memories?"

"No. Not yet. I'm afraid to discover anything else. I'm not sure I want to return to that life."

"Like I said, let's just cross that bridge when we come to it. No decisions need to be made yet. Each day as it comes."

Sipping my coffee, I relished in its ability to kick me where I needed it. I sighed, not expecting Harley to even notice. Apparently when it came to me, he didn't miss much.

"I'd ask if you've had a rough morning, but it's still fairly early, so, tough night at home?"

I swung my eyes to him, wondering why he'd ask me that. For a moment, I thought I should tell him to mind his own business but truth be told, he'd hit the nail on the head. Nick had told me last minute about a business trip which would have him out of town for a few days, maybe a week. I'd almost told him not to come back.

"It's complicated."

Arching an eyebrow, he riveted me with a sultry stare. "It's none of my business, but I'm here if you need to talk. I know not a soul, so your secrets are safe with me." He gifted me with a sensational smile, causing me to take a swift breath. My eyes were on his mouth, secretly wondering how soft it would feel on mine. Such finery deserved a certain amount of credit and worthy attention, no matter how wrong the idea was.

"My boyfriend the workaholic is the problem. It's finally beginning to piss me off." Glancing around, I made sure others nearby hadn't overheard me.

"You deserve better." Such simple words, yet not easy to facilitate.

"I don't know what to do. We've been together two years. I know he cares about me, but he loves his job more."

Not expecting his hand to reach across and take mine, I practically choked on the coffee after attempting to swallow. Coughing roughly, garnering a few stares from the people facing us, I attempted to pull away. He held on fast, gripping my fingers. "Hey. Just because you've been with the guy a while doesn't mean you have to stick around if you're not happy." Then he said something out of left field, which embarrassed me. "Is he good in bed?"

This time I did wrench my hand away. Why would he ask that? Besides the fact that Nick and I had a sex life bordering on non-existent, I wasn't comfortable discussing it with a man who could pose for an Italian sculpture.

"I'm not answering that." Stealing my eyes away, I suddenly found my Styrofoam coffee cup interesting.

"I'm sorry. I shouldn't have asked. It's just that, a woman of your caliber should have a man who worships her in and out of the bedroom."

That got my attention. My mind conjured up images of Harley idolizing my body. I couldn't hold his gaze while my brain played its own R-rated movie, but I could sense him still watching me.

"We're not here to talk about my sex life. I brought you here to offer some company in what is going to be a very boring day." Pushing my chair out to stand, he caught me off guard.

"Wait!" His arm stretched out as if to stop me. "Don't go. We can talk about something else. Anything. Just…sit with me."

This guy knew how to stop me in my tracks. He only had to plead for my company and I caved. God. Talk about a pushover.

Settling back down, I placed my cup on the table, watching his body relax slightly. "Fine. I have five minutes."

With the clock ticking, suddenly neither of us had anything to say. It's not like I could ask him questions about anything. There were no answers he could give me. Instead, he watched me while he drank, his chiseled forearms garnering too much of my attention. Veins popped in odd places. Even with his dark features, the fine hairs on his arms were light. His fingernails were neatly manicured, although they could do with a cut. His rounded fingers looked perfect for caressing. Shaking my head, I gulped my coffee.

"Do I make you nervous?" he asked.

Hell yes! "Of course not. Why do you ask?"

"Well, for one, your pulse is hammering in your neck. Secondly, your eyes won't hold mine for longer than two seconds. And thirdly, your hands are shaking."

His heat burned me even from the other side of the table. The walls were closing in.

My physical body betrayed me on every level. Scanning the room, I noticed other women admiring the view too. Such a sight to behold—any female would be blind not to notice.

"The coffee here always does that to me." Such a weak excuse. Blind Freddy could see through it.

"Bullshit." He grinned amusedly. "Just admit it, Mac. Deep down inside, you crave a man who can offer you more than a tepid relationship. You've had *barely warm* since your virginity got popped. The reason I make you nervous is because I have something you want. There's no shame in it."

I didn't like being analyzed. The truth glared at me in frightening reality. Harley's words couldn't have been truer, but I wasn't going to boost his ego even further. Standing, I offered him a tight smile. "My break is over. I need to get back to work. What will you do all day?" I couldn't stay another minute with the direction the conversation kept traveling. My coffee could be finished in the ICU.

At only eleven a.m., the day would drag for him, but I had other responsibilities to take care of.

He shrugged. "Can't really go anywhere looking like this. What do you suggest?"

"Well, I guess you could hang here. There's a television and magazines just inside."

"Dressed in scrubs?"

Shrugging, I didn't have any other options for him. "If anyone asks, tell them the truth. You're a patient without clothes."

I bid Harley farewell, relieved to be out from under his thrall. Walking back to ICU gave me just enough time to clear my head and focus on what needed to be done for the rest of the day.

***

By six p.m. exhaustion and anxiety had taken hold. Nick still had no idea about Harley coming home. The evening would be interesting, to say the least.

Upon returning to the patient lounge, I found Harley slumped in a chair, asleep. He had the place to himself.

I walked over and nudged him awake. "Harley?"

Lifting his head, which sat at an odd angle, he gaped at me with bleary eyes. "Hmm?"

"It's time to go."

He straightened and peered around the room as if getting his bearings. "It is?"

"Yeah. You must have been asleep a while."

His stomach gurgled loudly, causing me to laugh. "Come on, we'll grab something to eat on the way home."

I'd changed into a pair of jeans and a light zip-up hoodie with a tank underneath. Clothes I kept in my locker. Harley's intense scrutiny of me didn't go un-noticed.

"Wow! You look different out of uniform."

I threw him an amused smile. "I'm just a regular person."

"I know, but after only ever seeing you in your

nurse's outfit, it's weird to see you in jeans."

"Get used to it, buddy. I'm a casual girl. Jeans and shorts. That's me."

"No complaints here," he said as he walked behind me a tad too close. If I had x-ray vision, I imagined his eyes to be fixated on my butt. My hoodie covered my waist but failed to fall further. The jeans I wore were rather fitted because they were made of stretch denim and were my all-time favorites. If I could, I'd wear them to work. I let him ogle as I led the way through the maze of University Hospital, the only sounds from either of us being me saying goodbye to co-workers.

We made it to the staff parking lot. By the time we arrived, I noticed Harley wincing.

"You okay?" I asked, unlocking the doors using the remote.

"Yep. Just not used to walking so far."

"The exercise will actually do you good," I offered, climbing into the driver's seat of my late model Shelby Mustang, my dream car.

Harley followed and turned to me with a surprised look on his face. "This is yours?"

"Absolutely. Isn't she a beauty?"

Shaking his head, he chuckled. "I never pegged you for a muscle car kind of girl."

Securing my seatbelt, I fired up the engine, loving the sound of the 500 horsepower V8. I gave it a little gas, showing off a bit. I wasn't a grease monkey by any means, but the power under my fingertips stirred a wild side in me. Male and female heads always turned when I stopped at traffic lights or drove through town. She stunned passersby with her gun-metal gray paint and chunky tires.

"Buckle up." I grinned madly at him, backing out of the lot and easing onto the main road.

"Nice ride, Angel. She sounds amazing." He nodded, a little bit of awe on his face.

Pride flooded me, knowing a guy like Harley would appreciate my baby's attributes.

"Doesn't she? I saved up for three years to get her. She's my pride and joy."

I felt his eyes burning into me as I indicated to turn into Neo Papalis, the best pizza joint in Ann Arbor.

"Do you mind if I order for you? Seeing as though you probably won't remember what pizza you like?"

Peeking over at him, he dragged his gaze away from me and checked out where we were. "Ah, sure. I guess."

"Trust me. You'll love the BBQ Bianca."

"Right now, I feel like I could eat the trash from out back, I'm so hungry."

"You're in for a treat then." I chuckled.

After ordering and driving the five minutes to my apartment, nerves began ratcheting up a notch. Having the hulk of a man beside me in my home had me struggling to find oxygen. I'd have to loan him some of Nick's clothes until we could get some new ones. Essentially, I was taking in a homeless man with no ready cash and no belongings.

Grateful for Nick's car being absent, I climbed out and led my protégé inside, stalking into the kitchen. "Do you want a shower before you eat? I'll get something for you to change into."

"Nah. I'll take one after dinner. My stomach is crying out for sustenance of some kind. I skipped lunch today."

"Oh. You should have asked a nurse for something to eat. They would have grabbed you a sandwich."

"It's all good. It just means I'll enjoy the pizza all the more."

My heart was galloping along at having this god in my kitchen. His presence filled the small space, causing me to fumble with the cupboard to reach the plates.

Heat shrouded my back, and without turning, I could feel Harley behind me. A large hand reached up and gripped the handle, covering mine, causing me to shiver at the contact. His skin felt warm and surprisingly soft. Breath blew across my ear as his deep voice lit me from the inside. "Let me help you with that."

I couldn't move or speak while cocooned inside his wrap-around body, jammed against the counter. His scent, mingled with freshly laundered scrubs, coated my nostrils. I let him open the cupboard, and with his free hand he took down the crockery, pausing a moment too long. I swore I heard him inhale sharply before stepping back.

"Do you want to eat in here or the living room?" he asked quietly.

I couldn't turn yet. I could still feel him not too far away and I didn't trust myself in that moment. My body betrayed me with the tingles shooting to my breasts and the heated mess between my legs. I needed a moment. Gripping the edge of the counter,

I ground out, "Living room. I'll be there in a moment."

I heard him pad away after a few heartbeats.

Get it together, Mac. You asked him to come home. You need to harden up and ignore any and all sensations he brings about while he's here. Things will only end badly.

Inhaling deeply, I steeled myself against my raging hormones and almost ran down the hallway, diving into Nick's drawer and pulling out a pair of sweats and a tank, before strolling into the living room to join Harley. I tossed the clothes down beside him.

He had three pieces of pizza on his plate, chowing down on one. "This is so good. You were right." Swinging barely a glance at the sweats and shirt, he offered, "Thanks."

Trying hard to ignore the BBQ sauce glistening on his defined mouth, I cleared my throat and took two pieces, sitting on the chair opposite him, placing much needed space between us.

"I told you. People drive from miles away to eat these. It's my once a month treat. I try not to overindulge."

Scanning my body from top to toe, he pioneered a trail of heat with his eyes, a slow, indolent grin forming. "It looks like you take good care of yourself."

How could he tell? I had a pair of jeans and a hoodie on. My jeans were skinny, but still.

"I try. Work is so demanding, sometimes physically, but more so emotionally, so I find if I'm in good shape, it helps."

"What got you into nursing?" he asked casually, taking a king-sized bite of his last piece of pizza. He could stack the food away quickly.

Happy to talk about neutral subjects, I answered, "It was a no-brainer. Since I was little, whenever anyone took ill, whether it be a person or animal, I always wanted to take care of them and make them better. I don't think it's something you become. I think it's something you are. I hate seeing people sick. I want to comfort them and ease their suffering."

Harley paused his chewing to study me. His pupils distended and a crease formed above his nose as if frowning. It wasn't a frown as such, though. More like my words affected him.

"I don't know how you cope when you lose people all the time. My memory…where my comrade got killed; I felt the pain as if it were real. It gutted me."

Glancing away, I thought about my answer. "I don't always. It's hard. We lost someone after you got moved to the ward. I keep needing reminders that we can't save everyone."

Dark orbs drilled into me, churning my stomach with nervous flutters. He looked into me, unspeaking. Deep and penetrating. I could almost hear the cogs of his mind turning. I wanted to be able to stare back, but if I did, I knew he'd consume me. He shook his head briskly and stood, reaching for the sweats, about to pull his scrubs down when I stopped him.

"Wait! Let me turn around first."

I swiveled, heat searing up my neck into my

cheeks as I pictured his ample legs and thighs bared before me. Squeezing my eyes shut, I heard fabric rustling and then a gentle sweep of the sweats being pulled up.

"Ready!"

Facing him again, I gulped to see him without a shirt. My Lord, he could restart hearts with that physique. Whatever he'd done in his forgotten past definitely involved weight training. Nick's sweats were a tad too snug but I wouldn't complain. Hell, I could almost see every lump and bump!

Look north, Mac. Damn it. Find his face and ignore the rest.

He must have licked his lips because they were moist and plump, slightly parted. He studied my reaction to seeing him half naked. Had I sold myself out? If my burning cheeks were anything to go by, I'd say he knew damn well what went through my mind.

Reaching for the shirt, I stretched out to hand it to him when the front door opened. Nick.

I pivoted toward the door, watching Nick's face turn from emotionless to surprised, and then suspicious. Eyes flattening to slits like his mouth.

"Hi Mac. What's going on? And why is this guy half-dressed and in my sweats?" He didn't attempt to come closer, but held his position two feet from the doorway. I could see how it looked.

He watched me before turning to Harley. I felt like I'd been caught red-handed doing something I shouldn't. Swallowing the sudden unfounded guilt lodged in my throat, I attempted to explain.

"Ah, Nick, this is Harley. He's a patient of mine

from the hospital." I rose and walked over to him. "Can I talk to you in private?"

He glared at me, his body language portraying agitation. Dropping his briefcase, he motioned to the hallway without responding further, glowering at our guest.

I shot a glance to Harley, who sat back down and gave me an "I'm sorry" look.

Stepping into our bedroom, I shut the door and turned to Nick.

"I was going to discuss this with you but you're never home, and well…I never got a chance. Harley arrived in the ICU with no memory. Total amnesia. He's still a John Doe. I took care of him. He doesn't even know where he lives."

Nick daggered me with a look, as if he could garner my next words. My gut somersaulted.

"He had nowhere to go. I—"

Before I could continue, Nick cut me off. Quick on the uptake, he knew me too well. "So you told him he could stay here. Of course you did. And how is he a John Doe, yet you call him Harley?"

"It's a long story—" Once again, he didn't allow me to finish.

Combing a hand across the back of his neck he scowled. "Jesus, Mac. You can't just bring stray people home as if they are some forlorn dog or cat. You don't even know the guy. He could be a criminal."

He had a valid point, but in my own defense, I argued, "I've hardly seen you over the last few days. The opportunity never arose to tell you. With work and you pulling an all-nighter, I didn't want to bother you. I promise it won't be for long. Just until we can figure something else out."

"I can't believe you would do this! You know I bring work home with me. How am I going to be able to focus with someone else here?" Gritting his teeth, he surprised me with his next words, "Especially a guy who looks like that!" His hand flew out, pointing at the wall in the direction of the living room.

"What are you saying?" My voice rose an octave, on keel with Nick's. Could he be jealous? Did he really notice Harley when most times he failed to see me?

"I'm saying, you don't just bring a random dude home to live with us and expect me to be okay with it."

His anger fueled my own. Hissing between my teeth, attempting to keep Harley from hearing, I seethed, "Maybe if we actually spoke, I would have asked you first. I never see you. I'm practically living on my own. Even when you are home, I'm alone. I'm doing the right thing and I'm sorry you don't agree with me."

His eyes flashed and his jaw knotted. "I'm done having this conversation with you. I work hard for us. I've told you this."

"There is no *us* if I never see you!" Tears were forming but I didn't want to let him see them.

Nick turned, storming into the closet, pulling out a bag and throwing it on the bed.

"What are you doing?" I asked.

"I'm packing for my trip tomorrow. I'll stay at Jason's tonight. I expect our guest to be gone by the time I return."

"I can't believe how unreasonable you're being."

He huffed as he walked backwards and forwards from the closet to his bag, throwing things in and then stalking to the bathroom to collect his personal items.

"Why do you have to stay at Jason's tonight?" I couldn't believe it. I'd always been home at nights, waiting around for him to finish work, eating dinner by myself because he'd had to stay back. Falling asleep on my own so many nights I'd lost count, and this one thing I felt I needed to do and he was carrying on like a child.

I didn't attempt to stop him. Perhaps we really were strangers. Shutting the bedroom door, I strode down the hallway to find Harley had switched on the television, thankfully. He'd also put the tank on.

He looked up at me when I moved to sit on the couch. "Everything okay?"

Shaking my head, I whispered, "He's leaving."

Harley sat up straighter, "As in *leaving, leaving*?"

"I don't know. He's going to stay with a friend tonight. Tomorrow is his business trip. He wants you gone when he gets back on Wednesday." I knew Harley wouldn't be ready to leave by then, so I may as well face facts that my relationship with Nick resembled a pile of rubble.

Harley scooted closer until his meaty thigh touched mine and he placed an arm around my shoulder, pulling me into his side in a gesture of comfort. "I'm so sorry. It's my fault. I'll leave."

"No!" I shot back. "It's not your fault. This

situation has been brewing for a while. It's only come to a head tonight. Please. Don't go. You have nowhere else." Being alone would not be good for me.

His nearness helped quell my hurt and anger, the large arm providing a barrier to Nick's hostility.

Hearing the bedroom door slam, I pulled away from Harley and shifted to the end of the couch. Nick appeared, bag in hand.

He uttered not a word and didn't glance our way as he stormed to the front door, opening it and throwing it shut behind him. Seconds later, he tore out of the driveway.

Burying my face in my hands, I let the tears show themselves. The craziness of the past week had taken its toll, and more to the point, the harsh reality being that I believed my relationship with Nick was unsalvageable.

"Hey. It's gonna be okay." He pulled me gently into his oversized chest and embraced me in a bear hug. "Shh. I got you." Letting my guard down, I sobbed into his shirt, or rather, Nick's shirt, angry that my relationship had reached this point. In the past I'd been too clouded by routine to see things clearly. It wasn't until Harley's arrival that I'd begun to question things...namely, my feelings for Nick. Sometimes familiarity proved safer than stepping into the unknown. I also felt disappointed in myself for putting up with something less than I deserved. My friends had tried to warn me but I had never listened. Nick's screeching tires shook some sense into me.

I became all too aware of Harley's thumping

heart beneath my tear-stained cheek and his rigid muscles bunching under his shirt. He had an air of danger about him that both frightened and tempted me.

Sniffling out the rest of my melancholy, I pulled myself together and inched away, strangely saddened that I couldn't remain ensconced within his shield.

He swept the pads of both thumbs under my eyes in a gentle arc to wipe away any residual tears. I focused on the emotion playing out across his face. Distress played out over his features.

"Better?" he asked with a choppy voice.

"Mmm hmm." This time he caught me in his web of heat. I had to mentally remind myself to breathe.

"I'm sorry about Nick," he crooned.

I wondered if he meant it. He'd already voiced his opinion about me being able to do better.

"Are you?" I didn't mean it in a hostile way but more to garner the truth.

Breaking his hold on me, he looked down to his lap. "I won't lie to you. The guy doesn't know what he has in front of his nose. He literally chose his job over you and for that, I'm not sorry of the outcome. But I am sorry you're hurting."

"I guess sometimes it takes other people to wake you from whatever relationship coma you've been in." Did he pick up on my innuendo?

His sculpted lips elevated at the corners but didn't progress into a full smile. "And who might those other people be?" His eyes traveled all over my face, resting on my mouth. Puffs of breath wafted over my skin. My blood sizzled. He was too close and yet not close enough. The chemistry between us morphed into its own entity, and try as I might, I couldn't fight it.

Before I could take my next breath, a large hand gripped the back of my neck, drawing me forward and onto his mouth. The softness of the kiss took me by surprise. I expected it to mirror the rest of his tough exterior.

He led and I followed, happy to dance to his tune. Clutching his head, I pulled him in harder, wanting more but unable to pinpoint what *more* was. A rumble transferred from his throat into mine, his hand on my neck, massaging the area beneath my skull. His other hand came to rest at the base of my spine. We were so close, I could feel him hard and ready at my groin.

Like a warning bell chiming in my subconscious, I drew myself away from his clutches, heaving from near delirium.

"We can't. It's not right. Nick's just gone. We haven't actually broken up yet." Even though in my heart, I knew I couldn't go back to the way things had been, jumping into a kiss with Harley bordered on cheating. Damn my rational side. I'd never been kissed so thoroughly. My body craved more, but I had to put a stop to my hormones taking over.

I couldn't look at him. His breathing sounded louder than mine.

Standing and racing down the hallway to my bedroom, I shut the door and slid down onto the carpet, wondering what the hell I'd just done. I wasn't the type of woman to succumb to someone so easily. My boyfriend had literally only shut the door before I locked tonsils with Harley. Having him in my home when the energy surrounding him called to me like a double shot caramel latte could prove to be my biggest challenge.

Dragging in a few deep breaths, I rose and changed into my sleep shorts and tank, climbing into bed, needing the oblivion of sleep to knock me out.

Chapter Fifteen

Harley

I kissed Mac. The word kiss didn't seem enough to describe what we'd shared. How could you put into syllables a moment whereby the world around you disintegrated and you were left with nothing but the sensation of your five senses on overload? Touch. Taste. Smell. Hear. See. All working together in perfect harmony until you became only those five things. Even now without her in the same room, she lingered.

Christ! Had I taken advantage of her vulnerability? What must she think of me?

Was she upset? Should I go to her? Perhaps I need to give her time.

Forcing my body upright, I strode to the bathroom, needing a shower to help douse the flames licking my loins.

Before I reached it, I hovered outside the room opposite, wondering if I should check on her. Did she hate me? My hand moved to knock, but at the last minute, I dropped it and shuffled into the bathroom. I'd give her some space for now, but I needed to apologize. She brought me into her home to help me find out my identity. I owed her a huge amount of respect and a great deal of restraint.

When I finished washing myself, I wrapped a towel around my hips and moved to the spare room, noticing it's sparseness but happy for some privacy. The double bed with taupe sheets and a chocolate, furry blanket folded across the end, beckoned me. I prayed nightmares wouldn't find me tonight before I settled under the cool sheets on my back, closing my eyes and resting my hands on my stomach.

Danger lurked. My highly tuned senses told me as much but my body disobeyed. The soldier in me, the part that never backed down, turned the corner into the dank, dimly lit alley. I'd exited The Avenue nightclub in pursuit of a suspected terrorist. Tipped off from my superiors about an alleged bomb planted within the establishment, my sole focus was set on a suspicious dude who'd entered with a rucksack and exited without it.

After ordering the club to immediately evacuate, I pursued a person of interest. My Glock rested firm in my hand, safety off. Garbage perfumed the air from the overflowing dumpster against the wall of the club as I stealthily stalked deeper into the long, narrow passage. My skin prickled as my grip on my weapon tightened. The warnings to flee grew stronger the further I became entrenched in the haggard channel. A noise to my right had me spinning and aiming, my finger on the trigger. My stance mimicked that of a warrior, poised and ready for battle.

A plump rat scurried out from a stack of crates piled up like a haphazard skyscraper. Breathing out and only letting my guard down minutely, my head detonated with pain before darkness seized me.

My arms and legs thrashed about, something hindered my limbs as I fought off the nightmare. Unlike the first memory, this time I'd been the prey.

Hands fumbled at my shoulders, but a killer instinct drove me. Fight or die. My arm burst free of its restraint, lashing out.

"Ugh," my attacker grunted. Not manly but more feminine. "Harley! Stop! Wake up!"

Where had I heard that voice before?

Brightness flashed, causing me to open my eyes, transporting me to a different reality. One where I wasn't being attacked. Swiftly sitting up as best as I could, I noticed my sheets were a tangled mess around me.

Upon further inspection, I realized Mac stood just out of arms reach, a horrified look on her face and blood dripping from her lip.

Full awareness hit me with icy clarity.

I'd hit her. Shit! Shit!

"Angel! I hurt you." Swinging my legs over the bed, I moved to stand, but she shuffled backwards in fear.

I deserved the fright holding her body rigid. Seeing her face drawn and her eyes panicked kicked me through the goalpost of remorse.

"I'm sorry...your lip. I didn't mean to."

Stumbling over my words, my heart felt like it dangled from a meat hook. I noticed her eyes were now huge and not stuck on my face, but rather my groin. Peering down, I forgot I went to bed naked.

"Damn," I spat, sitting back down and covering myself with a sheet.

"It's all right. You were asleep." Even in fear, she played down what had happened, making me feel shitty. I wasn't sure to what degree my anger could escalate, but with absolute clarity, I knew I would never intentionally hurt her.

"No!" I demanded. "It's not all right. Come over here and let me take a look. You're safe. I promise." My outstretched hand wasn't enough to placate her.

She studied me with indecision. Her face had paled and her arms were folded tightly across her torso.

Shakily, she asked, "Another memory?"

Frowning, I nodded. "I think I know what happened to me."

That had her taking a step forward. "Really?"

"I got shot in an alley, right?"

"That's the information we were given by the paramedics and police."

"I remember looking for a guy there. A criminal." Giving her a sincere, apologetic smile, I stood and attempted to close the gap between us, pulling the sheet around my middle.

"I'll be back in a minute. I need to take care of my lip." She turned and quickly strode from the room to the bathroom, where I could hear her opening the cabinet and turning on the faucet, effectively ignoring my admission.

I hated myself for hurting her. I'd rather harm myself than bring any pain to Mac. She'd been nothing but nice to me and didn't deserve my wrath, even if it occurred without my knowledge. Just what had my life consisted of? After two intense, disturbing dreams, it became clear that I hadn't lived an average life. Returning to the end of the bed, I sat and waited for her.

When Mac returned, she carried the clothes I'd shed in the bathroom. I'd left them on the floor, mindlessly.

She threw them on the bed, silently demanding I put them on. Not wanting to argue, I dressed and patted beside me.

"Please. Sit. You want to help me piece together who I am? Well, this new information might lead to that."

Casting a fleeting look toward her, I noticed her moving forward. The bed dipped as she sat on the edge, but she came no further.

Happy with that, I retold her my dream, leaving out nothing. She remained quiet throughout, consistently focused on me.

When I finished, I waited.

Silence ensued for a minute or so, and then she spoke. "What if we went back to the alley? It may trigger a memory. Something you've missed. Are you sure you didn't see your attacker?"

"Positive. He came at me from behind and must have hit me over the head with an object, hence the amnesia. He obviously put a bullet in my chest to finish me off. Luckily, I don't remember that part."

"But you remember the guy in the club? Could

he be the one who knocked you out?"

It sounded plausible. Perhaps the police could draw up an identikit image. Since it would be Saturday tomorrow, we could both go to the station and fill out a report.

"We'll go into town first thing and tell them everything I remember. It's not much, but it's a start."

Reaching for Mac's hand, I entwined my fingers with hers, noticing how small it felt. "Thank you. For everything. I don't think I would have made it if not for you. You're too kind."

She softened and squeezed my hand, sending tingles into my wrist and up my arm. "You're welcome. I want to see you as the person you've always been."

My mind battled with the thought. "What if you don't like that person? What if he's not good?"

Turning to fully face me, she placated me with her stunning eyes, which crinkled at the corners. "But nothing will change with your memory. Amnesia doesn't turn you into someone else. Not inside. You already are a good man. Just one without a past."

She didn't grasp the full volume of my meaning but I kept quiet. One step at a time.

Mac moved to get up, but I held her hand fast. "No. I couldn't get you to stay in the hospital, but I'm begging you here and now. Please don't leave me. I don't want to fall asleep alone."

I couldn't read her expression. She'd carefully masked her emotions. Instead, she leveled me with a watchful stare as if thinking hard of her answer.

Finally, she exhaled loudly. "Fine. Just for tonight, and no funny business. You keep to your side and I'll keep to mine. Deal?"

"Deal." My smile broke free and my shoulders slumped with relief. Just her presence alleviated my brittle nerves. Having her beside me would do. For now.

Climbing back under the covers, I lay on my back, my peripheral vision allowing me a glimpse of her long, bare legs as she climbed in beside me, settling on her side away from me.

Rolling over, I faced her, keeping enough space between us for her to feel safe. For the first time since waking up in hospital, my fear of the dark vanished as I breathed in her scent while drifting off.

Chapter Sixteen

Mac

Had I left the heating on last night? My temperature resembled molten lava. And had I grabbed the life-sized teddy bear Nick had given me when we'd first started going out? I remember seeing it sitting in its usual corner of the room last night. My limbs were tangled around something large with a soft covering. Definitely not fur, though.

Prying one eye open, awareness found me in a millisecond. Slivers of light seeped in from the edges of the pale blue curtain, allowing my sight to take in the scene. My head lay nestled in the crook of Harley's arm, which draped around me protectively, and one of my legs had wedged between his with my foot locked under his ankle.

Sucking in air, I became keenly aware of a rigid bulge at my knee. Shit. Had he awoken? I couldn't look. Listening to his breathing, I found it to be slow and regular, as if in sleep. If I moved I would stir him, but I couldn't remain with his morning wood nudging me.

After falling asleep last night, Harley had remained quiet. No further nightmares. A good sign. But when had I turned over and wrapped myself around him? I didn't even do that with Nick.

Nick hadn't woken up hard like Harley since we first became an item. He had always risen before me to get to the office early. The longer I remained clinging to this beast of a man, the more screwed I'd become. I needed space.

Lifting my head, I eyed his profile. Lips slightly parted, lashes brushed out across his lower lids. Spiky hair, sticking up at odd angles. Nothing feminine about him. Definitely all male.

Very gently, I lifted my arm from across his torso, carefully observing his eyes to make sure they remained closed. Disentangling my leg would be tricky. I twisted it to cause the least amount of movement possible and pulled it free. Harley's breathing remained steady.

Relieved, I lifted the sheets away and twisted my body in order to rise, but only made it a short distance. A large, calloused hand gripped my arm.

"Where do you think you're going?" his voice oozed out sleepily. Too damn sexy for my liking.

Pivoting my torso, the sight of his sleep-filled, bedroom eyes had me take pause while my heart palpitated. I coughed to dissipate the breathless sensation, ashamed that I reveled in his touch so much.

I...uh...coffee?" Could he see the nervousness clinging to me like a cobweb? His lips pursed, one corner lifting as if stifling a grin. He knew. Speaking of mess, my face and hair must have resembled a homeless person, so I pulled out of his grip and stood.

"Black, no sugar."

"I remember." Almost out the door, I stopped as he asked, "Mac?"

"Hmm?" It took a moment to gain the courage to turn back around to face him. He had propped himself up on both elbows.

"You said my name in your sleep." This time his lips did extend into a disarming smile. All American white teeth, too perfect for their own good.

Crap! Had I said his name? I searched his face for any sign of deceit but found none.

Damn. I couldn't remember what I'd been dreaming of. Obviously not Nick.

"Uh, you must have been hearing things in your sleep." I clutched at straws, desperate to escape his presence.

Racing into the hall, I heard him laugh, followed by, "I wasn't sleeping, Angel."

There wouldn't be a repeat of last night. I would be sleeping in my own bed from now on. I didn't need any further distraction from Harley or him cockily pointing out my faux pas while asleep. So I'd dreamt of him. It's not like I could remember. That didn't mean anything sexual. I could have been having a normal conversation with him. To a guy though, hearing a woman say their name in sleep was a huge ego boost, no matter how innocent it might be.

Turning the coffee pot on, I listened as I heard the shower start, glad of the reprieve for a short while. I needed to focus on what needed to be done today, and that included our visit to the local police precinct. The sooner Harley got his memory back, the sooner both our lives could return to normal. Did I want that? I wasn't so sure. What did I want? It wasn't my life with Nick. Not anymore. I'd wised up. Or woken up. One of the two.

Once the coffee brewed, I got comfortable on the couch with a bowl of cereal. The shower switched off and my wayward mind had a field day conjuring up images of a hot, wet, naked Harley stepping out onto the bathmat. His body was typical of a soldier—buffed with zero body fat. Nick's clothing failed to disguise Harley's sinewy physique. It merely acted as a safe buffer between us. Having a front row seat to his naked chest and almost naked groin earlier had only confirmed the fact. I remember how hard he'd been and the feel of his erection, weighty and primed, under my knee. The bastard had been awake the whole time.

I'd never been with a man so ripped. He had an eight pack! Not that I'd been counting. "Penny for your thoughts."

I jumped in fright, almost spilling my coffee as it sloshed in the cup. "You scared me."

"Sorry. Hang five and I'll grab a coffee then join you."

Seeing him fully clothed both pleased and irritated me. Having something to look at besides the back of Nick's head when he worked in our bedroom had me wanting Harley to ditch clothes altogether. I'd never tell him, of course, but it was my wicked little fantasy.

In reality, I'd need to get him something else to wear while we were out. I'm sure Harley wouldn't want to keep wearing Nick's stuff. It screamed *weird* seeing him strut around in my boyfriend's clothing. Maybe ex-boyfriend.

I had to ask myself the question as to whether I'd even want Nick back when Harley moved out. I didn't want to go back to what we had. There would need to be some drastic changes for me to consider it. And even then, the grass was beginning to look greener on the other side.

Quite simply, I craved *more*. More fire. More passion. More…everything. My dull and boring existence thus far had led me here.

"So. What time did you want to head to the station?" Harley sat beside me on the couch, taking up way too much space.

Shrugging, I offered, "I'll finish breakfast and take a shower, and then we can leave." Picking up my bowl from the coffee table, I held it up to him. "You want some?"

His eyebrow lifted. "Some?"

"Cereal?"

"Oh. Nah. Coffee's fine."

Suddenly things seemed awkward. Swallowing a chunk of oatmeal, I decided to grow a pair and broach the subject of sleeping arrangements.

"Harley, about this morning…"

He looked perplexed. "What do you mean?"

Had he even realized I'd been wrapped around him in bed?

"Ah, how long had you been awake before you grabbed my arm in bed?"

Willing him not to say it, I cringed inside.

Stifling a smile by placing his hand over his mouth, his eyes crinkled at the corners, giving him away. "You mean when you had your hands all over me and called out my name?"

"Pfft. I did not have my hands all over you, and saying your name in my sleep meant nothing."

"Tell yourself that all you want, but at some stage during the night you needed a strong male body to snuggle into, and I'm guessing you knew it wasn't Nick. I mean, come on! It's not like the guy has time to work out or anything."

Wasn't that the truth? Nick had an average build with little muscle to show. The hours he spent working hindered any chance of exercise.

"Cocky?" I goaded.

"Just telling it like it is."

He really enjoyed the banter and a part of me did too.

"So. Did you like waking up to a real man?"

Oh my God. He did not just say that. Talk about ego.

Rising to my feet, I turned my back on him so he couldn't see the flush I knew must be gracing my hot cheeks.

"Finish your coffee. Grab a shower and we'll head out."

***

At the precinct we were led to a small room off

the reception area and were greeted by a Sergeant Michaels.

"So, you're the John Doe we found in the alley?"

"Correct, sir."

"Glad you're making a full recovery." The middle-aged man, balding on top with weary blue eyes, smiled.

"Physically, I'll be fine. Mentally, well, I'm still trying to figure that out. It's why we're here. I've been getting snippets of memory back through my dreams."

"Oh? You sure they're not just dreams?"

I looked at Harley, who met my gaze at the same time. We had a silent moment. I'd said the same thing when he had his first dream at the hospital.

Shifting in his seat, he said, "No. I'm definite they're not. Everything seemed…familiar."

We'd explained to the officers on the phone about Harley's amnesia, so they were up to speed. Whether they believed the whole amnesia thing or not, I couldn't be sure.

Pressing *record* on a portable device, the sergeant nodded to Harley. "Go on."

I remained silent as the dreams were retold. No one could conjure up anything so realistic, surely. They had to have come from the deep recesses of his mind.

When he finished, we both sat eagerly, waiting for Sergeant Michaels to speak. "We can call some contacts we have tied up to the military and CIA. See if they can come up with anything. The trouble we might face is if you were Special Ops, there may be no record of your existence."

Come again?

"What do you mean? How can there be no record? A birth certificate must exist somewhere." My whiny voice sounded alien. I hated to think of Harley as a ghost.

"Some segments of the CIA operate off the grid. Covert operations and such. They're invisible for a reason. If what you told me is a memory, I'd bet my right leg you're going to have all sorts of road blocks getting information. We'll do what we can from this end."

Harley cleared his throat and lifted one foot up onto his other leg. His nerves blended with my own. "So there's no way to find out who someone is, if technically they don't exist?"

"Like I said, I'll contact some men in the industry. Nothing's guaranteed. Information isn't handed out freely. If you keep remembering things, that's gonna go a long way to solving the mystery. In the meantime, our sketch artist, Jared, will draw up an identikit and we'll see if we can get it circulating."

Blowing out a long breath and rubbing the top of his head, Harley glanced over at me. He looked lost. Reaching over, I squeezed his upper arm in a gesture of comfort, feeling the rock solid muscle of his bicep.

At least Sergeant Micheals took Harley's word and agreed to investigate a little. We had no one else to help us.

"What's the best number to reach you on?" asked the sergeant.

Cutting in, I said, "Mine. Harley doesn't have a

cell."

"Harley?" The cop's eyebrows rose in question.

"Ah, yeah. That's the name I've given him. It's better than John Doe."

Nodding and smiling, he jotted that down. "Fair enough. I'll be in touch if we find out anything." Holding out his hand to Harley, the men shook hands and then I followed suit. "If you sit tight, I'll go grab Jared." The sergeant stood and moved quietly out of the room, closing the door.

I risked another peek at Harley. He cut an imposing figure. All hard lines and testosterone. He must have sensed me looking at him because he focused on me with his usual intensity.

"I feel like we've wasted our time." He huffed, squeezing his hands open and shut as they rested on the table.

Needing to placate him and offer some hope, I clasped his hand. "This is the first step. It's going to happen. We just need to be patient."

"Angel, I may not know much about myself, but I do know I'm not a patient man. Not when it comes to something like this." He squeezed my fingers, showing no sign of letting go. He had a wicked grip. He only had me to cling onto. Someone real and willing to help. I'd be there for him as long as he needed me. In some ways I liked being needed. Apart from my nurse/patient relationships, I hadn't experienced it in a long time.

A stocky man with short mousy hair entered with a sketchpad and pencils. His roughened skin held a jagged scar, running from the edge of his jaw, down his neck, and under his collared police shirt. His light blue eyes looked jaded, as if they carried a burden no man should have to lug around.

"Morning," he cheered, failing to sound authentic.

"Hi," Harley and I both chorused together.

He sat opposite us and placed the pad and pencils on the table before gathering our attention.

"Okay. You ready to do this?" He gave Harley an encouraging half-smile, picking up a black pencil.

Harley nodded once.

"I need as much detail as you can give me. Hair, eye and skin color, facial features. Any significant abnormalities or extras we might need, such as tattoos, piercings, etcetera."

Sighing beside me, I still kept hold of Harley's hand, watching his focus leave the room and return back to the night at the club.

"The guy wasn't American. Dark hair. Messy around his ears. Arab."

Jared paused, his eyes lifting from the pad. "You sound pretty sure."

"I'm sure. I don't know how or why, but I'd bet my life on it."

A shiver chilled a path from my feet toward my heart. To hear him so definite about the nationality of the guy who could have been involved in Harley's shooting had my brain a flurry of random thoughts. His dreams of being in the armed forces, and now connected with an Arabian man began to paint a picture in my head. One of danger.

I barely heard Harley recounting more of the guy's features as I wondered just how much trouble my new house guest attracted. Whatever he'd been involved in had brought itself to my town. Shit.

***

Once outside, I waited for Harley to speak, not wanting to stir his emotions. His rigid gait posed a picture of a warrior. Or a soldier.

He didn't say a word until we were on the road, heading home. "I can't fucking believe if I've been operating off the grid, I may never find the answers I seek. My best guess is they'll catch the asshole who shot me first, and there's no way in hell he'll talk." He hammered the heel of his hand half a dozen times onto his thigh. I couldn't blame him.

He'd never used the F-bomb before. Not that I minded too much. Soldiers would surely use that type of vocabulary every day.

"I hope his contacts can lead us to someone who can help."

"I'm not liking my chances, Angel." He white knuckled the seat in frustration. I couldn't begin to imagine how he felt. How many other soldiers off the grid had suffered amnesia in the past? I'd say, not too many.

Parking out front of my garage at the apartment, Harley led the way to the front door. He paused a few feet away, craning his neck at an odd angle as if attempting to listen to a hushed noise.

While he did that, although odd, I put my key in the hole, twisting it, only to find it already unlocked. Strange. I'd secured it earlier. Had Nick returned?

Before I could push open the door to find out, Harley gripped my wrist.

"Stop." He pulled me away from the door, and with a commanding tone I hadn't heard before, he barked, "Stay here. Don't move."

Okay. What the hell? Why had he ordered me to stay put? And why did he look like a bomb about to detonate? With no time to speak, he'd thrown open the door wide, striding in like he'd just switched into a different person. Darker. Confident. Bossy.

My pulse kicked into high gear, a tendril of fear curling in my chest.

Cussing ensued, the volume dwindling the further into the apartment Harley went. Alarm had me clutching my throat.

If something had happened to my apartment, I needed to know. Ignoring his order to stay put, I stepped inside the open door, letting loose a strangled cry. "Oh my God!"

The living room had been trashed. Pictures on the walls hung askew, one smashed on the carpet. The sofa had been overturned, cushions splayed in spots of the room like a dot to dot, as if they'd been strategically placed there to create a sick picture. My wild, horrified imagination threatening to send me into a tailspin.

Harley stalked down the hallway toward me. "I thought I told you to stay outside?"

Not answering his gruff chastisement, I held both hands to my face. "Why? Who would have done this?"

Harley stopped in front of me, arms stiff at his side. "That boyfriend of yours angry enough to pull this off?"

"Nick? No. He might have left in a huff, but he'd never do anything like this. Heaps of his stuff is still here."

It wasn't Nick. I didn't care what Harley thought. Whoever had done this had clearly been sending a message, or had been searching for something. Maybe they'd been scoping out the place, waiting for us to leave.

I tried to think if I had any enemies besides a pissed off boyfriend. A disgruntled patient? That didn't make sense. None of them knew where I lived. Records at the hospital were confidential.

Strong arms wrapped around me and I fell. I fell into him, needing the support because my legs were about to give way. I'd been violated in a personal way.

"I'm sorry I growled at you. I'm not sure where that came from, but my instinct was to find out if someone was still in the apartment and hurt them real bad."

His chest surged and fell. His arms tightened around me.

"Military impulse?"

"Maybe. All I know is, I had the urge to destroy. As if someone had taken over my body and mind. It felt instinctual."

"Little snippets are returning to you. It's a good thing." For him. I wasn't so sure about me. Nick's biggest outburst had been when he came home and found Harley bare-chested in our living room. I hadn't ever experienced intimidatingly uptight men thus far.

Lifting my face up to meet his, I found him staring into space. Jaw set. Teeth grinding loud.

Whispering, he answered, "What if it's not?"

***

The police arrived ten minutes later. We hadn't touched a thing in case we tampered with evidence. The notion of someone entering my home, invading my privacy and touching my stuff cut me deeply and messed with my trust and sense of safety. What if they came back? What if they were watching us now?

"So you have no idea who might have done this?" questioned the young officer, who had a female partner at his side.

"No. I keep to myself. I work as a nurse, and when I'm not working, I'm here. It doesn't make sense."

The female piped up, "What about you?" She jutted her chin out toward Harley.

His eyes widened a fraction. "I…uh…I'm not sure."

Both officers looked at each other, then to me and back to Harley with sudden interest.

He proceeded to explain his situation, realization suddenly dawning on me too as I recalled my scattered thoughts at the precinct earlier.

Harley would have amassed enemies as a soldier. But being a ghost, how would anyone even be able to find him? If the police weren't able to locate personal information about him, how would an enemy be able to? Unless of course that enemy had been the person to attack him in the first place and had been watching and waiting the whole time.

God. My life was spiraling downwards with no end in sight. Suddenly I felt as if I'd jumped into an episode of a crime show. What the hell had I gotten into by bringing Harley home? Nick had been right all along. We didn't know the guy. It would appear he came with a lot of baggage, and to what extreme, I didn't know.

"It may have been an unlucky, random event, but we'll do a drive around the area and see if we notice anyone or anything suspicious. In the meantime, be alert, and if you discover anything at all, no matter how small, give us a call." He handed Harley his card and walked through the apartment, eyeing the damage. "Anything missing?" he asked when he returned.

"I'm not sure yet. We haven't checked. We called you guys right away."

"Have a search through stuff and let us know."

"Will do. Thank you."

"We'll do a quick dust for fingerprints in here." He motioned around the room. "I doubt we'll find any, but its protocol."

"Can we begin cleaning up this mess? I asked.

"Yep. I can't see why not. You got insurance?"

"Um, I'm not sure. I'll have to check up on that." Nick may have taken out insurance when we moved in, but I didn't have any.

The policeman nodded, getting back to his task at hand. Harley grabbed my hand and pulled me down the hallway to my bedroom.

"You all right?" He dropped my arm and put

both hands on my shoulders, piercing me with sympathetic eyes.

"I don't know. I guess. I'm just glad you're here." A simple thought crossed my mind. If Harley hadn't come home with me, none of this would have happened. I shook it off. It didn't matter now. I needed to deal.

The next thing I knew, strong arms pulled me against an ample chest in a fierce hug. I didn't want to move a muscle. Knowing Harley went into survival mode upon entering the apartment appeased me somewhat. Even if he couldn't remember his training, I began to think, if it came down to it, he'd fight to protect me and himself.

"If the person who broke in has anything to do with my past, I'm so sorry they've followed me here. I should do us both a favor and leave, to keep you safe."

I should have agreed with him, but knowing I'd be on my own carried a decent amount of fear. If the person came back looking for Harley, it would be disastrous without him.

"I'd rather wait until the suspect is apprehended. I won't feel safe until then."

His lips rested on the top of my head, his breath on my scalp. I inhaled his calming scent and burrowed into his chest.

"Then, I'm sleeping in here with you again. I'm not leaving you vulnerable. If the asshole comes back, I'd rest easier knowing you were near. I can't protect you in another room."

As much as having him sleeping in my bed a second time had me all sorts of anxious, it also relieved me to know I'd have the hulk of a man as a barrier to any intruders.

"Fine, but no funny business."

"I wouldn't dream of it, Angel." Winking, he turned to inspect the damage to my room. "Let's get this mess cleaned up."

Once we had the mattress on the bed, clothes folded into drawers, and personal items replaced, I relaxed a little. Nothing had been taken so far, or nothing I noticed. Harley's room didn't have much in it to begin with, so straightening it up took only a minute. When we'd finished the bathroom, we headed back into the living room. The officers were finishing up, so we bid them farewell, locking the place up when they were out the door.

Reality began to set in as I gaped at the disaster my living room had become. My shoulders shook and the first tears fell. I'd never had anything like this happen before and it unsettled me more than I cared to let on.

Harley heard my sniffing and walked over to me, taking my hand and dragging me into the kitchen, which was the only room relatively unscathed. He sat me down at the kitchen table. "Coffee?"

Nodding, unable to speak, I watched him set to work, wondering how he coped so well.

Allowing myself a couple of minutes to settle, I asked, "What's your take on what happened? Do you think it's linked to the attempt on your life?"

He had his back to me, but I didn't miss the buckling of his back muscles as he fought to answer my question. Perhaps he didn't need to. His body language spoke volumes.

"It would appear so. Who else could it be? It's not like you've made any enemies."

Pausing with both hands gripping the edge of the counter, I watched his head sag down in defeat. "Have you got somewhere else you could stay for a while?"

"What? No. This is my home. Why should I leave?"

Lifting his head and spinning to face me, his startling eyes had lost some of their luster. "I just think you'd be safer away from here."

"Do you think they'll come back?"

"It's hard to say. I'm not sure what they were looking for. If they were after me, why not wait until I'm actually here? Why trash the place?"

"To send a message. They want you to know they've found you again."

"This is all so screwed up."

I clung to the mug of steaming coffee he handed me. We had a job ahead of us out in the living room…to clean up smashed glass and put right the shambles. We both looked like we needed the hit of caffeine to revive us as we chugged it down.

"I'm not sending you out on the street where you're an open target. I'll get an alarm fitted."

Joining me at the table with his own mug, we eyed each other. "That might be a good idea. I'll take you to and from work until we get this guy or guys."

My eyes dilated. "You remember how to drive?"

"Just because I can't remember my past, Mac, doesn't mean I don't know how to do stuff. Of course I remember how to drive."

I wasn't sure how the whole amnesia thing worked. I hadn't had to deal with any other patients in a similar situation.

The rest of the morning and most of the afternoon we spent, putting back the jigsaw pieces of my apartment, making it look halfway decent again. I'd need to replace a couple of pictures, and we'd thrown out a lamp, but apart from that, most of the mess had been fixable.

The lock on the door remained intact, so whoever had broken in had picked it. I'd need to see about getting a deadbolt fitted too.

All the times I'd been home alone while Nick worked, I'd never worried about my safety. It scared me how easy it had been to break in.

For dinner I fixed us a stir-fry with chicken and cashews, which Harley devoured.

"You're a great cook! This is delicious!" he murmured with a mouth full of food.

Laughing at his gluttony, I couldn't help but like cooking for someone and have them eat with me. It didn't happen often.

For myself, I often made easy meals and didn't take the time to fuss. To have him enjoy it thrilled me.

"Thank you. I actually like to cook. I just haven't done too much of it in the past couple of years. You tend to slap together something basic when eating on your own."

"Well, if you keep feeding me food like this, I won't be in a hurry to leave." His dark orbs swam with regret, as if those very words had him wishing at some point he didn't have to. Once we found out about his life though, chances were someone would be waiting for him to return home.

Who would protect me if the criminal who'd broken into the apartment hadn't been caught by then?

A level of unease sat low in my belly and would remain there until the threat was removed.

Perhaps my thoughts became words written on my face, because Harley asked, "Will you be okay on your own when I eventually go? I mean, if you don't get back with Nick?"

Running my finger around the cup rim absentmindedly, I pondered that question. I'd practically lived the last two years alone, but in my mind, I still knew Nick lived with me. Now, his belongings were scattered around the place, and while some of his items still remained, his lingering presence had vanished.

"I could eventually move in with a friend." My voice faded out on the last line.

"But?"

Wasn't there always a but? I liked this apartment and its proximity to work. The fact it didn't have stairs worked in my favor. Plus, my work friends were on changeable hours like me. Our shifts altered every couple of weeks, so I'd end up living with someone who would be sleeping through the day fifty percent of the time and vice-versa. I may as well stay on my own and get used to it.

"I'll cross that bridge when I come to it."

Finishing his last forkful, having eaten every scrap of dinner I'd served him, my ego sang with joy that he loved it. To see an empty plate after cooking made my inner chef feel worthy. I didn't consider myself a whiz in the kitchen, but I knew the basics.

Harley collected his plate and took mine, which I'd pushed away, leaving a small portion. He proceeded to load the dishwasher, which added to my growing list of *likes* about my John Doe.

Remembering I had a bottle of wine in the fridge, and even though we'd both only just finished our coffees, I offered, "Wine and movies?"

Turning to shoot me a blinding smile that had my libido kick into overdrive, his eyes folded at the corners. "Sounds perfect."

And so we got comfortable on the couch while Harley let me choose the first movie.

"You seriously want to watch *Fast and Furious 7*?" His question held both mirth and awe.

"I like the movies. Why? What were you expecting me to choose? *Pretty Woman*?"

"Well, yeah. You look like a *Pretty Woman* kind of girl."

"Maybe looks can be deceiving," I shot back, half teasing, half not.

He gifted me once more with his astounding smile before chuckling, "Maybe. You continue to surprise me, Mac."

Harley reached across to the coffee table and poured us both a glass of red, handing me mine along with eyes of fire. I almost missed grabbing the glass as I flailed in the two pits of smelted coal.

I burned and drowned in equal measure, a thick cloud of lust forming around us. Perhaps the events of the past twenty-four hours had my need for escape higher than normal. I wanted to forget everything for a while. My fingers wrapped around the delicate glass, but I wasn't out of his clutches. The pad of his thumb brushed across my knuckles with all the gentleness of butterfly kisses. My hand began to shake and I knew I'd end up spilling the wine over both of us, so I broke our staring contest and gently pulled my hand away, willing my pulse to settle.

Every inhale of charged air had me hyper aware of him. I daren't look back or my body would sell me out.

I pressed *play* on the remote, hoping the introductory music might cut through the dense atmosphere. No such luck. His energetic field had already merged with mine, and while we were in the same room together sitting way too close, it ruined me.

I didn't want to feel anything, but my body had other ideas. I could no more control my raging hormones than I could alter time.

"Angel…"

I stopped him in his tracks by holding up the palm of my hand. "The movie is about to start."

Did he feel the fireworks too? How could he not? The room had become a swirling vortex of pheromones.

Swigging the entire glass of wine in one go, I welcomed the bitter burn and quickly filled up my glass a second time. All the while, he kept me under heavy scrutiny. Knowing those damn, disarming peepers were trained on me didn't make things any easier.

Suffice it to say, even though I'd seen the movie before, I barely heard or saw any of it. Instead my mind overthought everything about him. I couldn't work out why he affected me so.

An hour into it, I chanced a peek at the towering inferno beside me and caught him still staring at me. God. Had he even looked away?

"You're not watching the movie," I squeaked.

"It seems familiar. I must have seen it," he rumbled, imprisoning me in a visual showdown.

"Oh. So you don't want to watch it again?" The fact that another snippet of his memory peeked through failed to excite me as much as his fiery stare.

"I prefer to watch you." His tongue swiped his lower lips, whether for my benefit or not, I wasn't sure.

I choked on a swallow, causing me to cough. Needing to distance myself from Harley before I did something I might regret, I stood and rushed to the bathroom, locking myself in.

Everything within me was on high alert. Giddy with sensation and anticipation, my breathing had turned choppy. Forcing a glance into the mirror, I wasn't surprised to see a pair of flushed cheeks and dazed eyes.

My willpower had all but crumbled. It hung on by a thread. How would I sleep with him in my room tonight? Ugh. Perhaps I should just let events unfold. Fighting the attraction proved exhausting.

What advice would Char give me? Go for it? Stop betraying Nick? I doubted it would be the latter, knowing her stance on my non-relationship.

Breathing steadily for a minute, I rubbed my face and returned to the living room, stopping short of the couch real quick. No!

Chapter Seventeen

Harley

The thread of restraint I'd been grasping onto had frayed and snapped. She wanted me and I wanted her. A blind man could feel the sexual attraction in the room. I could give her what she needed. The erection I'd been sporting the whole way through the movie hadn't waned. My balls were hitched up tight and ready to let loose.

Mac had run. Scared. I couldn't blame her. She didn't know me. *I* didn't know me. But I reacted to her on an intimate level. My angel. My savior. The light to my dark. She fed a part of me I knew held only black. It festered inside. Caustic. Walking in to find her apartment trashed had unlocked a reaction in me that felt like home. A familiarity with my being. The warrior. My soldier status began to feel like more than just a title.

The sudden heat building in the room inspired me to throw my shirt off. The cooler air licked gently over my beading skin, easing the burn only minimally. I needed a cold shower.

Mac appeared without me having to turn to confirm it. I could feel her. My tight muscles contracted further in my back and neck, causing my wound to stretch and burn.

Each second ticked by in excruciating increments, labored breathing the only sounds.

"What are you doing?" she whispered.

Attempting to hold back from ravaging you was what I wanted to say, but I didn't. Instead, I offered a, "It's hot in here."

My fingers squeezed and opened on my thighs. I had to put an end to this madness.

Rising, I rounded the corner of the couch to find her wide eyes focused on my chest, mouth agape, legs wobbly. Thankful I wasn't a waif of a man, I stood tall and proud of my physique, watching her eyes blacken as I approached and stopped in her personal space.

"Stop." She attempted to iron out her guilt but failed.

"I don't want to stop. I've been pulling myself back all evening. I can't do it anymore. Just one touch, Angel. Just one kiss. Let me taste you."

Whimpering and backing away did her no good because she only served to reach a dead end. The wall hugged her back while I guarded her front. Towering over her, a protective instinct leapt forth, causing me to cocoon her in with both my arms bracketing her head.

"I…uh…Nick. He's my boyfriend." She could tell herself that all she wanted, but I knew better.

"He's not your boyfriend, Angel. He's your

housemate. That's all. Someone to share the bills, but not your bed or your heart. You're so damn lonely. Let me fill the hole. Christ! Do you know how good we could be? You're so eager and yet so righteous. Stop denying your body what it wants. What it needs."

I still wasn't touching her but I may as well have been. She scorched me like fire and brimstone. I could see the drumming pulse in her neck. The heavy swell of her chest caused by thick breathing.

"I can't." She still hadn't looked at me. Stubborn woman.

"One kiss. That's all. Nothing more."

I wanted so much more, but I wasn't about to force her.

With painstaking slowness, her chin lifted and her eyes hooked onto mine. She had me in a second. Totally. She showed me everything I needed to see and more. I pounced, primed and ready.

Keeping my hands free, my lips were the only things to dive in. We were physically joined by mouth only, and yet she filled the gaps. Around me. In me. With a desperate groan I ransacked her mouth and she let me, giving herself over to what we both couldn't deny. Heaven came to greet me as she opened up like a spring bud touched by the morning's first rays of sunshine.

A long, satisfied whine rattled from her throat into my mouth, where I swallowed it eagerly. My angel had wings and she flew me to the stars. Kissing soon wasn't enough. I needed more. Much more. My earlier promise disintegrated into thin air. No longer could I keep my hands away.

Pressing my chest into hers, feeling the hard pellets of her nipples dig into my pecs, I let my hands roam free. One shifted down her back to the ass I had been dreaming about, awake and asleep. Nothing in my head could compare to the real thing. Two perfect globes, perky as if just hand-picked from a peach tree.

My other hand stroked up her side, seeking another mound. One with its small monument standing high and proud.

The shirt she wore became a hindrance, so I bunched it in my fist and began lifting it, only to be stopped.

"Harley!" Mac could barely breathe. "You said just a kiss."

"Do you want just a kiss or do you want my hands on you?"

Lowering my head, I pulled out her bottom lip and sucked on it. In response, she pushed her chest further into mine. Desperation oozed from her pores and still she held onto her strong mind, which screamed at her to be a *good girl* and stop. I could see it in her eyes. A pleading glare mixed with lecherous indecency. This woman teetered on the cusp of stepping over to the wild side. She needed a little push.

"Tell me!" I ordered, feeling the dark corner of my soul seeping out, wanting clearance to possess me.

"Touch me!" Her eyelids shuttered over the tumultuous green sea, leaving me with only crescents of hazel. Her defined, plump mouth opened, funneling the air she needed to douse the fire burning inside.

Lifting her shirt and tossing it aside, I marveled at her cleavage jutting out of the barely there bra. Had she worn the lacy scrap of fabric for me? My ego would like to think so, for it clapped with glee like a kid at Christmas who'd just unwrapped the biggest present under the tree.

Both my hands leveled at her breasts, cupping the volume, each thumb brushing across a nipple. They barely moved they were so damn hard.

Her pulse erratically raced like mine. Needing more of me on her, I bent and took her neck in a flurry of lips, teeth, and tongue, nipping at the erogenous zone below her ear.

"Aargh." The long shaft of her neck held taut, her face angling away so I had full rights. A hint of perfume lit the taste buds under my tongue as I absorbed it into me. A fine wine couldn't be this good.

Two delicate hands dug into my biceps, bordering on pain, but I welcomed it. I hadn't felt more alive since I'd awoken with no history.

Dragging a shapely leg up to my hip, I kneaded her ass cheek, pulling her pelvis in line with mine.

"You feel so damn good, Angel," I purred into her ear, working her lobe with my swollen lips.

She simpered once and then her hands left my arms to forcefully thrust into my chest. "Harley. Stop! I mean it. I can't do this!"

Growling, I slammed a hand into the wall, arching my neck back to find her face. The glazed, disoriented look had been replaced with determination.

Everything in me screamed out to ignore her and move in for the kill. If only I hadn't looked into her eyes and viewed the questions written there. Damn. Her pulse throbbed. My lips were tingling.

I watched her shut down and put her wall of restraint up as she fought for control and much needed breath. I'd affected her without a doubt, but the moment of intense lust had passed for her.

Willing my darkness to fade out, I pushed off the wall and skulked away, down the hall to the bathroom. Slamming the door, I turned and rammed my head into the wood a few times to gain some clarity.

I needed to reel in my hunger and settle down before I slammed my fist into the mirror above the sink.

Jesus! What happened to me? Who the hell had I turned into? A hothead with no morals. Part of me felt like a dick for overstepping my boundaries with Mac, but the other part sat on a mountain of disappointment and rejection.

A small piece of my psyche spoke to me. It informed me I wasn't used to being denied anything. I liked to be in control. A leader. One who gave orders. With Mac, I didn't have that. I careened from a high altitude with no safety net or parachute.

Switching the water on in the shower, I stripped and let the pounding spray knock some sense into me. I stayed rent free in my nurse's home. It would be in my best interest if I contained myself. At least until she gave me the green light to proceed further.

I hated the void in my head that wasn't providing

me with any answers about my nature. It was like being a fully programmed and charged computer but a virus had wiped the hard-drive. I had a recycle bin to retrieve information but I couldn't access it willingly.

The cold water did the trick. My frustration had receded to a niggle as remorse swept in. I shouldn't have stormed away from Mac. She didn't deserve that. I owed her everything. Lathering myself up before rinsing and drying off, I knew what I needed to do.

Chapter Eighteen

Mac

Downing the rest of the wine in the bottle after regretfully wrenching myself away from Harley's hot clutches, my libido began calming down. I'd done the right thing by disengaging completely. Now, fully clothed again and without him in the same room, the tension had eased.

I wasn't ready to jump into bed with a practical stranger, regardless of how much my body cussed me right now. Or regardless of how honest it felt. I'd regret it in the morning. My emotions were all over the place after Nick stormed out and my place had been trashed. A night of heated passion with my John Doe wasn't going to change those two things.

Hearing the water switch off, I took the empty wine bottle to the trash bin in the kitchen and quietly padded down the hallway to my room, not bothering to switch the light on or change. Climbing under the covers, I faced the window and closed my eyes, knowing sleep would elude me for at least a couple of hours, but I was hopeful nonetheless.

My rationality had kicked in, and thank God it had, or I'd be writhing against the wall, totally lost to him, instead of cowering under the covers listening for any sign of his anger.

Ugh. Most women wouldn't think twice about which side of the equation to choose. One look at the bulk of the man drying off in my bathroom and they'd be throwing themselves at him. Begging for his attention.

The bathroom door opened. Harley's feet shuffled softly on the floor for a few steps, stopped for a beat, and then began until he neared. Had he been considering sleeping in the spare room? I didn't blame him.

Leaving the bedroom door ajar, he pulled back the covers and climbed in beside me, wriggling restlessly before stilling. My breathing had slowed at the mountain of warmth beside me, even with the air laced with tension. While earlier had been purely sexual, the new layer sheathed around us held buckets of discomfort.

"You awake?" he asked with a rumble.

"Mmm."

"I apologize about earlier. I got carried away."

"I did too. I'm sorry. With all that has happened, I can't cross that line just now."

"I know. It won't happen again."

I wanted it to happen again. Just not tonight, and maybe not even tomorrow. I liked the thought of him wanting me in that way. I hadn't felt needed by a man in such a long time.

Silence ensued for a good five minutes before I

spoke, hoping he hadn't fallen asleep.

"Harley?"

"Yeah?"

"Maybe I want it to happen. Just not yet."

The bed dipped as he moved and then I felt a partition of heat at my back. Thick legs tucked into mine, and his chiseled arm bracketed me against his chest from behind.

Squeezing my eyes tightly, I forced in air, wondering if he'd heard what I just said.

"Sleep, Angel."

He wouldn't let any harm come to me, regardless of what had happened earlier. Having him swathed around me, all brawn and protectiveness, heart a running tempo, I truly felt safe.

I slept.

***

"Mmm. Trudy…"

What? My brain had a hard time keeping up with my eyes as they opened to a voice. The only understandable words uttered were a woman's name. Harley no longer cocooned me, so I turned to find out more.

Eyes closed, head thrown back a little on the pillow, the hulk of a man lay flat on his back, covers thrown off to his waist. His lips were parted as if preparing for more dialogue.

Clearly in the middle of a dream, I became alert, hoping he might reveal some more about his past that we could use to find out his identity.

"Nice. Hahaha. You're funny."

Did people actually laugh out loud while sleep-talking? It would appear so. Making a mental note of the name "Trudy," I waited for him to continue, but with a sigh, his head lolled to the side and he became silent again.

I now had a million thoughts running through my head and no way to slow them down. A twinge of unease sat low in my gut, twisting stronger at the significance of hearing a woman's name coming from his mouth while sleeping.

It could be totally innocent, but something about the way he'd groaned it out had me believing that his reverie wasn't so run-of-the-mill.

Thank goodness it would be Sunday tomorrow. Getting up for work early after broken sleep would hinder my ability as a nurse. I didn't do well on my feet all day after burning the midnight oil.

Listening to Harley begin to snore didn't help matters. Turning away from him onto my side, I fluffed my pillow and closed my eyes, hoping to drift off on a wave of fatigue...hope being the operative word. Sleep eluded me.

I could be lying next to a married man. What if I'd kissed someone's husband? There might be a woman out there going insane with worry over the disappearance of the father of her children.

The whole situation sucked. Imagine if she lived nearby, not knowing her man slept in another woman's bed a few blocks away.

If Harley passed her on the street, he wouldn't even recognize her.

My bad habits included overthinking. He may not even be taken. The fact that he dreamt about a

Trudy could simply be a case of a girl from his past, long gone.

Still, now that the seed had been planted in my head, it began to take root and grow.

At three a.m., I must have finally given in to the crushing fatigue. When I roused, the sun attempted to pierce through the curtains the next morning.

I could tell Harley wasn't beside me without even looking. He had a presence I could sense.

The sheets were tousled, with a slight indent in the mattress where his form had been. From the bedroom I couldn't hear any sounds.

Rising and throwing a robe on, I groggily padded out into the living room to find it vacant, but the smell of coffee hit me hard, alerting me to Harley's whereabouts.

As if sensing me enter the kitchen, he asked, "Coffee?" His naked back buckled under his taut skin. The back of his head rose as he stood gazing out the rectangular window above the sink. He wasn't admiring the view because it consisted of other apartment complexes bunched together in the area, their roofs a palette of different shades of the same color brown.

"Thanks. That would be great."

Should I bring up Trudy in the hope he'd remember his dream? And more importantly should I prepare myself for the information he might offer?

Pondering on the idea, I sat at the table and waited for him to pour my drink and hand it to me.

He didn't sit opposite me, but walked back over to the adjacent counter and leaned against it, facing me, both hands gripping the edges.

"Sleep okay?" His scratchy, deep voice caused me to shiver.

"I tossed and turned a fair bit. You?" I fished for answers.

"Like a baby."

Sipping my drink, I let my eyes drop to the table. My mouth moved of its own accord. "Remember anything about your past while sleeping?"

Out of my peripheral vision, I saw he stiffened further.

"Why do you ask?"

Chancing a peek up, I found his gaze pensive. His brown irises narrowed as his pupils grew.

Inhaling deeply through my nose, I came out and said it. "You said a woman's name. Trudy."

Pushing off the counter, he grabbed the back of his neck and paced in front of the table. His teeth ground hard together.

"I...I knew her. Well. It wasn't much, but we were at a beach. Playing around. Chasing each other. She laughed, flicking water up at me as we rang along the edge. I caught her and picked her up. Carried her in deeper and dunked her real good. She came up still laughing. And then..."

I hadn't moved. Hanging onto every word. Needing to hear it but not wanting to.

"What happened next?"

"We were kissing." He stopped with his back to me, breathing hard.

Internally cursing him for saying the words, I tried to act nonchalant. "Do you think it was recent?" A sliver of jealousy wove its way through my toughened heart. It only lasted a moment but it made me feel as if I swam in a sea of uncertainty.

He dipped his head back and stared at the ceiling. "I guess. But it could have been an old memory. An old girlfriend."

True. Funny that he should have that as one of his initial memories though.

"Sometimes we dream of people we haven't even met and yet they are familiar to us. Could it have been a case of just a random girl?"

Perhaps hope gave me one final push before I lost it completely. I had no right to garner that hope. I wasn't his to lay claim to. When he eventually got back to his old life, I'd merely be the woman who took him in and helped him when no one else had. Maybe even a friend.

I didn't like that the word *friend* brought a further ache to my chest.

Sipping the rest of my coffee, I wasn't sure what else to say. Harley's drink was going cold.

"I knew her. I remember her long blonde hair blowing in the sea breeze, sticking to her face. Her large blue eyes, deeper than the ocean we stood at. I can't explain how absolute the memory is."

He stopped and faced me as if realizing his mistake. "Mac...I'm sorry. I don't need to be telling you this."

"I asked." I wish I hadn't. He genuinely had feelings for the woman. Anyone could see it. The milk from my coffee began curdling in my gut.

He stared at me for a beat too long before changing the subject, briskly.

"What are you doing today?"

"What?"

"Today? Do you have plans?"

"Ah, just some washing. Apart from that, not much."

"Feel like spending the day doing something? With me?"

"Are you sure that's wise, considering someone wants you dead? We'll be open targets."

Pondering the truth of my words, he replied, "We'll go somewhere with lots of people. No one would be silly enough to make a move with loads of witnesses. Plus, I have a feeling if it came down to it, I'd be able to protect you."

Witnessing his hostility upon entering my ransacked apartment, I didn't doubt him, and I needed to get out in the fresh air. "Oookay. What did you have in mind?"

Chapter Nineteen

Harley

Being cooped up like a caged animal had my head about to implode. The risk of taking Mac out sounded in my head like a gong, but I knew I could protect her against any asshole attempting to use her to get to me. We both needed a day out to chill and get our minds off everything.

"So," I prompted. "Where do you want to go?" Considering I had no clue where anything was, I would leave the driving up to her and the choosing of a location.

With a smile and a twinkle in her eye, Mac replied, "Summer Festival is on. Let's go into town and see what's happening. Plenty of people around to act as a shield."

"Awesome. Get changed and meet me at the front door in ten minutes."

I put on a pair of Nick's runners that were a size too small but would have to do, and some more sweats and a tee. I needed to get some clothes of my own, but with no money available, I didn't like to rely on Mac for my expenses, even though she'd offered. I had already encroached on her life without being a burden financially too.

Mac appeared from the hallway with her hair tied up in a ponytail and attire similar to mine, except she wore a white singlet top, showing off her slender neck and shoulders. It brought all sorts of lewd images to mind, testing my willpower as she brushed past me with a smirk on her face, opening the front door.

"Ready?" she called over her shoulder.

"Always," I huffed out, not necessarily referring to us leaving the apartment.

She shot back, "Even though you fill out Nick's sweats better than he did, we still need to get you some clothes of your own."

Adjusting my crotch, I kept my eyes away from her tight ass and breathed in the fresh air as we walked to her car.

The short ten minute drive into town failed to jog any memories, which disappointed me a little. I thought something might stir up an emotion or reflex, but by the time we pulled into a parking spot not too far from the center of Ann Arbor, not a thing had registered.

"You okay?" queried Mac with a furrowed brow.

"Yeah. I hoped I might remember something, but it's all good. Let's just focus on today. I'd like to forget about everything else going on."

Switching the ignition off, Mac exited, followed by me a moment later.

Being a Sunday, the streets were busy, and even

more so because of the festival.

"We'll have to walk a few blocks. I hope you don't mind. This is the closest we'll get." A sign read, **'McKinley Towne Center.'**

"Actually, a walk in the sun sounds great."

"I heard there's a circus. Do you want to check that out first?"

Her voice sang with excitement, and she had a bounce in her step as we began our walk. Mac appeared almost childlike.

"I'd love to see a circus." I really would. It sounded like something we could both lose ourselves in. And God knew, I needed that. After dreaming of a cute blonde woman kissing me and then having Mac swaying her hips beside me, I definitely needed a distraction.

We ventured down East Washington Street until we spotted the large white turreted tent in Burns Park.

Mac turned to me and gifted me with one of her brilliant cheek-splitting grins, which I couldn't help but return. The atmosphere increased threefold as we approached to purchase tickets, me suddenly realizing I'd be further in debt to her.

"It costs money. How about we just walk around and look at other things?"

Her look told me there would be no arguing. "Are you crazy? You don't want to see the circus?"

"I didn't say I didn't want to. It's just…"

Cutting me off, she held up a hand. "Stop. If it's about money, forget it. In the years I've been working and living with Nick, it's not like I ever went anywhere to spend it. Believe me when I say, I have some saved up."

"Still…"

"Shut it, Harley. We're going." With that she grabbed my hand and pulled me closer to the ticket stand, where she purchased two tickets.

Her determination brooked no argument, so I conceded.

The inside appeared bigger than the outside as we checked our tickets and found our seats. People of all ages lined the bench seats. The smell of hotdogs and cotton candy filled the air and I couldn't help but soak it all in. Excited children fidgeted, clearly anxious for the show to get underway.

We waited for another fifteen minutes before the presenter came out and introduced the one-man show.

Mac clapped and cheered, totally into it, causing me to beam at her enthusiasm. I could watch her all day rather than the circus, but because she had spent money on my ticket, I turned my gaze to the center ring.

The lone guy did all his own stunts and acrobatics. Clearly super-talented. He had everyone on the edge of their seats, even me.

I could feel Mac staring at me. She smirked when I turned to her.

"What?" I asked.

"It's good to see you enjoying yourself. You're really into it."

"I really am. Thanks for insisting we come inside." I placed my arm around her shoulder and pulled her in to me for a loose hug. Goosebumps pebbled on her arms from the contact, causing my ego to high-five. I'd always known I affected her as she did me, but she obviously wasn't ready to let her guard down any more than she had back at her apartment.

Letting her go, we enjoyed the rest of the show before stepping out into the brilliant sunlight.

After my eyes adjusted, I asked, "Where to now?"

"Fancy a coffee and a bite to eat?"

My stomach had informed me numerous times it needed food. And a coffee wouldn't go astray either. "Lead the way." I swept my arm in an arc, letting it settle in front of me.

Mac led me into a Chipotle Mexican Grill. It was roomy with a large food selection.

We both ordered chicken tacos and a couple of coffees before settling at a table by the front window.

"Anything from your past surfacing yet?" asked Mac, placing her purse on the table.

"Nah. Nothing yet, but we've only been to one place and I'm thinking the circus isn't somewhere to cause a flood of old memories to burst through.

Shrugging, she said, "You never know. Maybe your parents took you to circuses when you were a kid."

The word *parents* had my heart seize for a moment. Who were they? Were they still alive? Where did they live? They'd surely be frantic if they thought I'd come to harm and just vanished off the face of the Earth. It saddened me to think they'd be grieving.

"Sorry. I didn't mean to stir up negativity."

Taking my coffee from the waitress, I took a sip before answering. "You didn't. Not really. It's just…hard not knowing who your mother and father are."

Giving me a sympathetic look, Mac smiled. "I totally get it. That must be the worst part. But you have to remain positive that this is only temporary for everyone, and soon, we'll get you reunited with your loved ones."

She continued to amaze me in every way. Her support offered me strength and hope, two things I needed the most if I wanted to get through this. With her by my side I felt like I would be okay.

"I hope you're right."

After receiving our food, we ate in comfortable silence, watching the passersby out the window going about their day. I didn't feel like I had to indulge in mindless conversation with Mac. I hoped she felt the same way and wasn't ill at ease.

The tacos were to die for. The best thing I'd eaten so far in my limited bubble of an existence.

We both used the bathroom when we finished and I waited outside while Mac paid the bill.

"Do you feel like walking those tacos off? We can stop anywhere worthwhile on our journey. Maybe go into a menswear store?" Mac surprised me from behind as I stood gazing out at the crowds.

An uneasy feeling swept over me as I nodded and took a step away from the eatery. It became so strong I stopped briskly, leaving Mac to take a few more steps before she realized I wasn't walking beside her.

"Harley?" Her nervous voice took a backseat as all my senses came alive. Scanning the vicinity, I searched for anyone who looked suspicious. There were way too many people to reveal anything. Were my enemies nearby? Were they watching?

The person or people who attacked me could be lurking anywhere. Hiding. Waiting. I needed to be on guard, ready at any moment should they strike. Maybe it had been way too arrogant to assume I could take them on when I didn't know them. They'd already almost killed me.

A touch to my arm made me jerk hard.

"What is it? You look like you did right before we found my apartment trashed."

Seeing the concern light her eyes, I masked my anxiety and grabbed her hand, lacing her fingers through mine to help me ground myself. My intention had been to enjoy a day out with Mac and that's what I needed to do.

"Nothing. Come on. Let's walk." I'd be quietly on guard without causing suspicion.

She stared at me a moment too long before silently facing the front and walking back the way we'd come earlier.

We hadn't gone far before she asked, "Do you think someone's following us? Are we in danger?"

I didn't know. I couldn't describe the feeling. It wasn't so much a sensation like the one that had gripped me at her apartment but more like me being under someone's heavy perusal. She needn't be frightened, as it may pan out to be nothing more than my overactive imagination.

"No. It's nothing. Just a reaction to the amount

of people around."

Until I sorted it out in my own head, I didn't want to worry Mac.

"Hmm. Another snippet. You don't like crowds," she said more to herself than to me.

We wove our way through the throng of pedestrians with no destination in mind. As the minutes ticked by, I relaxed more. Mac's soft hand disappeared in mine. It felt so much smaller and it made me feel like her protector. I gave it a light squeeze and felt her return it.

Shoulders and arms brushed and bumped into us as they passed, so when I felt a hand on my arm and someone say, "Declan? Dec, honey is that you?" I became an ice statue.

Mac spun around at the same time I did, our fingers still entwined. Natural instinct had me shove her behind me in a defensive gesture.

Finding myself face to face with a woman who seemed vaguely familiar and with wide-eyed shock drawn onto her face, I faltered.

"Excuse me? Do I know you?"

At my words, she flinched, confusion taking place of her shock. Blue eyes centered on me and didn't let go. Eyes that had me shiver as if I were dead and someone had walked over my grave. Déjà vu washed through me and yet, my brain wasn't making any connection. She looked pretty. Really pretty. Clearly by her body language and the way she stood in my personal space, she thought she knew me. The crowds wove around us as we stood in the middle of the sidewalk.

"It's me. Trudy. Your wife."

A gun had gone off in my chest, dead center, causing me to stumble backwards into Mac, who stepped out from my shadow, taking up residence beside me. Her body stiffened, hands gripping her purse way too tightly.

"What?" Perhaps I hadn't heard her correctly. My wife? Glancing down quickly at my wedding finger, I found it devoid of a ring, but as my sight honed in on her left hand, I gulped back a curse at the small gold band, glittering in the sunlight. Shit. Shit. No. It can't be.

I didn't feel married, but how could I? My brain had shut down the vault that held all of my past. My gut twisted as I tried to see reason. She could be lying. My current self, hoped that were the case. But as my brain switched gears, a flash of memory exploded.

Recalling my dream from the night before, the blue eyes challenging me, and the flowing blonde locks blowing gently in the warm breeze were like a puzzle piece locking into place.

Trudy. My wife. Not my girlfriend. My fucking wife, and she stood in front of me waiting on some sort of recognition. I couldn't give it to her. Even with the familiarity I'd felt while asleep, this woman failed to ignite any sensation in my chest, connecting me to her. I must have had a detached and vacant look on my face, because she furrowed her brow and clutched her shoulder bag strap.

"You don't recognize me? What's going on, Dec?"

Dec? Declan? I shuffled the name around in my head, hoping to come up with a lick of awareness, but it fired nothing but blanks. She may as well have called me Bob or Tom, because Dec didn't register.

Now Trudy focused on Mac. For a moment, I'd forgotten she stood beside me. I looked between the two women, noting them size each other up.

"Who's this? And what are you doing back in town? I thought you were still on assignment?" Trudy added, motioning beside me. Her voice started to rise.

It annoyed me that I should have to explain myself to a stranger, but the suspicious gleam in her eye had me offering a vague response before changing the subject.

"Uh, this is my friend, Mac. Assignment?" I needed to find out more now that the only woman who could piece together my past stood in front of me. What assignment? A military one?

Refocusing on me, she nodded. "Yeah. Assignment. You've been out of the country, remember? Why are you acting like this? You're starting to scare me."

Mac remained a silent statue beside me, which I mentally thanked her for. I couldn't begin to imagine what ran through her head when mine throbbed with too much information.

Needing more than anything to speak with Trudy, I offered, "Can we go somewhere to talk? It's complicated."

Glaring at Mac again, she replied, "I bet."

I heard Mac shuffle her feet nervously. Our day out to have fun and forget all about her apartment being broken into had crashed and burned, but knowing I needed to hear Trudy out had everything else take a backseat. I hoped Angel understood.

"Fine, let's head back to Burns Park. We can talk there."

"Lead the way." She smiled hopefully.

I turned to Mac and nodded for her to come too. Disappointment cloaked her eyes, but she began walking with us. Finally, I'd get some answers.

Chapter Twenty

Mac

My chest collapsed in on itself. He had a wife. A life. One I wasn't a part of from this moment forth. I knew it would happen, but I hadn't planned on it being so soon.

Trudy had a pretty face. Gorgeous even. She'd been crestfallen to discover Harley hadn't recognized her. She had my sympathy. Put in her situation, I'd be the same. They were a beautiful couple. Watching them walk together across the road had me all kinds of knotted up. I shouldn't have felt that way, but I did. Harley, or Declan as Trudy knew him, epitomized the perfect male. Attentive. Intense. Warm. Funny. To think Trudy had already laid claim to him filled me with disappointment. I'd crossed professional boundaries and done something I swore I'd never do…become attached to a patient. For whatever reason, I'd grown personally invested in my John Doe, and now it would end in heartache. Silly. Silly me.

I should let them catch up. I should walk away. A part of me wanted to do that, but another part wanted to hear what she had to say. Plus, Harley looked at me as if he needed my support through this. I'd promised him I'd be there to help him, so I had to swallow the ache in my gut and do just that.

It seemed odd to think of him as Declan. Harley fitted him. Watching him walk with Trudy as I tagged along served to remind me that Harley had been created by me. An illusion. He wasn't real. Made through unforeseen circumstances, and now the bubble had burst. I'd lost him before I ever had him. The notion of him returning to Trudy's home and beginning a life with her caused all sorts of distress inside me.

I never should have agreed to take him home like a stray dog. I should have just let fate decide his future and stayed the hell away.

Watching his back muscles flex and relax, I turned my head to the side to avoid tormenting myself further. I'd felt those very muscles, hard and plump beneath my fingers. His hands in my hair, fine mouth devouring mine. God. Hands and a mouth that belonged to someone else.

Had I cheated with him? Technically I'd cheated on Nick, even if he had left in a fit of anger, causing irreparable damage to our relationship by never being emotionally available, but had Harley cheated on his wife when technically she didn't exist in his world?

He would never be Declan to me. I didn't know that person. I only knew Harley. They may be one and the same physically, but mentally they were separate people with separate lives.

Even if Trudy gave him the answers he needed, it still didn't mean he would remember anything.

How could he return to a life he had no recollection of? A woman he didn't know?

My day had gone to shit and it wasn't over yet.

***

Finding a seat in the shade of a goliath oak tree provided us with a certain amount of privacy away from the circus.

I sat on the end of the bench with Harley in the middle and Trudy on the other side of him. Being the tag-a-long, I resolved to keep quiet and simply listen.

"So here's the thing," Harley began. "The last memory I have is of following a guy out of a club and getting shot in an alley. I woke up in University Hospital with amnesia and don't even know my parents' names. Up until you showed up only minutes ago, I existed as a John Doe, or as Mac called me, Harley. No identification of any kind, which of course means I don't recall where I live, with whom, or what sort of car I drive."

I caught the look of sheer horror on Trudy's face and felt a little sorry for her. She hadn't played a part in any of this, and now sat beside her husband, who thought of her as unfamiliar.

If it were me, I'd be devastated.

Dropping her hand from her open mouth, she muttered, "Shit. No wonder you looked at me like I had grown two heads. You truly don't remember me?"

A tic in Harley's jaw grabbed my attention, along with the muscles in his neck forming a rigid line. "Pretty much." Turning to me, he looked lost as he faced her again and confessed, "I had a dream about you. Us. I dismissed it as a random snippet from a past girlfriend." He took pause and then almost whispered, "It was you."

Sensing the moment turning all sappy and emotional, I stood. As much as I wanted to be there for Harley, I could feel anxiety rise high in my chest. "Uh, I'm just gonna go grab a coffee and leave you both to it. I'll be back in ten."

As I turned to leave, Harley gripped my arm tightly, causing me to pivot around.

"Stay. Please?" His voice had a pleading lilt to it, like the one I had become used to in the hospital. "Stay" bled from his lips whenever I moved to leave him. His fingers bit into my skin and his face took on a panicked expression.

Chancing a look at Trudy, her big blue eyes had widened, her eyes flicking between Harley and his hand on my arm. She must be wondering where I fitted into it all. We hadn't discussed much yet, and already I needed to distance myself.

The way his gorgeous brown eyes drilled into me and his fingers held firm, I knew the sincerity in his request, so I quietly put my carcass back down to wait out what I knew would be an epic talk.

"Tell me everything," Harley ordered, turning back to face Trudy.

Crossing her legs, she let out a long sigh and proceeded. "Okay. Where to begin. Well, we met in high school and dated for a while. Nothing serious back then, and it fizzled out after graduation. We both went our separate ways. I went to college and studied business and you followed your dream of joining the military."

Veins in Harley's forearm protruded as he flexed his hand. Nodding in confirmation, he remained quiet as she continued.

"We met up again four years ago through a mutual friend. You were on leave and I had just started working as an event manager. After a couple of months of dating, you proposed and I said yes."

My eyes expanded at that. He'd asked her to marry him after so little time. It all seemed so fast.

"I did? We did?" Harley seemed as stunned as me.

"Mmm hmm. Just like that." She watched him to gauge his reaction, but I couldn't see his face.

His body tensed. Every piece of bare skin tightened.

"So…are we still married?"

The million dollar question. One I didn't want to hear the answer to.

"It's complicated."

"Complicated how? We're either still married or we aren't." His voice sounded like a drill sergeant now. All business and authority.

"We were separated, but had agreed to try and work things out." She shifted uncomfortably, her gaze sliding away.

"What happened? Why did we separate? And how long were we married?"

I wanted to know too. The word "separate"

spiked my interest threefold. They weren't together, even if legally they were still married. Maybe the situation wasn't totally screwed up.

"We were married three years. We had a short engagement. It was hard, though…you were always away on missions. I barely saw you…" Her voice trailed off.

Harley breathed in and out heavily for a minute as if to process everything. I still had questions I wanted to ask, but I didn't think it my place, so I kept quiet.

The silence proved a bit awkward until Harley spoke again. "My family. Where are they? Who are they?" His edge had sharpened. I could certainly imagine him barking orders to a team of soldiers in battle, swathed in weaponry.

"Your father passed away eight months ago. Your mom lives here in Ann Arbor. Not too far away." Trudy's nerves could be felt like a live entity. She obviously knew Harley far better than I. His reactions to things.

Gripping his neck, Harley gritted out, "Fuck! My father's dead? How?"

I touched his arm lightly, needing to offer support. He had mountains of information to deal with, and he'd need me to help him get through it. Two bombs had been dropped in the space of half an hour. Learning of a dead father when you couldn't remember what he looked like must be horrible. I squashed my selfishness and focused on providing comfort. Nurses were highly skilled in that area.

Without looking at me, he reached his hand over

and placed it on my knee, giving it a reassuring squeeze, settling me only marginally.

"I'm sorry. He was a great man. And so proud of you." I watched Trudy's hand come up to his shoulder in her own gesture of consolation, knowing she had every right to as his wife.

Removing my hand, I looked out over the park, wishing I could be swallowed up into a black void. This day had strayed from its course in a huge way. Little did we know of the outcome when we'd pulled away from my apartment.

"His name was Sergeant Andrew Harding."

Without missing a beat, Harley swung his head from his lap to Trudy. "He was in the military too?"

"Yeah. He's the one who got you interested in it. He was retired, but still had his finger on the pulse."

Declan Harding. He now had a moniker. An identity. It would serve to help us figure out more clues and fill in some of the blanks. Pfft. Us. Listen to me. There may no longer be an us. Harley may choose to let Trudy help him now. I might have to let go and get my own crumbling life in order.

"How did he die?"

"Heart attack."

Harley stole his gaze away from her and raised his head up to the sky, turning enough for me to see his closed eyes.

I wanted nothing more than to take him in my arms and steal some of his pain, but I guess Trudy wanted that too.

She moved to lean in and give him a hug, but he moved off the bench, gripping his hair. He growled and began pacing, agitation clearly running through him.

"Jesus Christ! My own father is dead and I can't fucking remember a thing about him. What he looked like. His favorite food. Talking to him! What my last words were to him. Did we even get on well? I have no idea!" he raged.

Trudy and I glanced at each other. She appeared as crestfallen as me at the fiasco.

I couldn't begin to imagine not remembering my family. People who had raised me and guided me. Loved me.

"My mother's name?" he barked, jittery and on edge.

"Beth. Bethany Harding."

His chest rose and fell heavily. He looked to me and said, "I have to go. I can't deal with any more knowledge. You right to get back to your car and home, Angel?"

Nodding, I muttered, "Where are you going?"

"I need to walk. Think things through."

Beginning to stride off without offering Trudy a goodbye, she called out, "Wait!"

Fishing in her purse, she stood and held out a card. "Here's my number. If you want to talk or visit with your mom, call me."

Watching her and then peering at her outstretched hand, he moved forward, slowly took the card, and stalked off.

I wasn't sure what to say or do.

Trudy eyed his retreating back. "I can't believe any of this has happened."

"You and me both."

Steeling me with her blue eyes, she whispered,

"Are you his girlfriend?"

Very doubtful at this point in time. There was no name for what we were, but girlfriend definitely wasn't it.

"No. I…I was his nurse. When he got discharged from hospital, he had nowhere to go. I couldn't leave him without a roof over his head, so I offered my place. Somewhere to stay until he got his memory back."

"He likes you." Her voice had a hint of resignation but mostly betrayal.

She loved him. They had been planning on getting back together. After spending half an hour in her presence, she actually seemed like a nice person. She must be hurting so much. I didn't want to add to it. I knew what I needed to do.

"Look, you don't need to worry. Now that we know you're his wife, I'll have him move out. I don't want to stand in the way of you reconciling. I didn't know."

The idea of handing him over hurt like hell, but I had no choice. I wouldn't be "the other woman." Why then did doing the right thing cause an ache in my chest?

"As much as I want that, I need to be realistic. He doesn't remember me. It would be like moving in with a stranger for him. Do you honestly believe he will agree to that?"

Syphoning in a deep breath, I shook my head. "Honestly, I'm not sure what he'll do. He needs to access his accounts and get some ID together, visit his mom. Pick up his car if he has one. Where was he living if you guys had separated?"

She dug into her purse and pulled out a notepad and pen, jotting down something. When she handed it to me, I saw two addresses. The first one being Harley's apartment, and the second, his mom's address.

"Thank you for taking good care of him. The least I can do is give you any information you need."

Smiling at her for the first time, I offered, "You're welcome, and I appreciate it." Pausing, I folded up the paper and put it in my pocket, going to say something but re-thinking it.

Trudy must have noticed. "What is it?"

"How long have you guys been separated?"

Thinking about it a moment, she replied, "Around twelve months. I've never stopped loving him, though."

And why should she? He had so many qualities I liked too. If distance were the only thing coming between them, I really didn't stand a chance. A shard of disappointment lodged itself deeply in my heart. My secret crush needed to end. Life would move forward and eventually I'd forget about my John Doe.

Wondering what to say next, I spluttered, "So where do we go from here?"

"Wait for Dec to calm down and see if he's up to visiting his mom, I guess. He'll need to access his bank account, and so on. I still have old records at home he can use. I'm not sure if he kept the account open once we separated, but it's worth a shot. If he needs ID, we can photocopy the marriage certificate." Thinking for a moment, she added,

"Oh, and his birth name isn't on any of his records. For military purposes. Being Special Ops and all." She gauged my blank reaction and then said, "He had nothing on him at all?"

"No. Whoever shot him could have taken his wallet. We don't know much at this stage."

"Well, for what it's worth, Dec was involved in some top secret missions I wasn't privy to, so the attack on him could certainly be linked to his military career."

I thought so too. It made sense. Which meant both our lives were in danger.

"Has anything like this happened before? An attack on Harley, er…Declan?"

"No."

"Is there any way we can contact a comrade or military boss to notify them?"

"I only know a couple of Dec's military buddies." She broke eye contact, and for a second her cheeks pinked. Not knowing what went through her head, I waited. After a moment she regained her composure. "Because it's all off radar work, the less partners, family, and friends know, the better."

Somehow we had to make contact. "Do you have the number for one of his buddies then?"

"I do, but as far as I know, he's still deployed." Retrieving her cell, she keyed in a couple of things. "Here. I'll give you Charlie's number. You'll have to explain who you are if you get a hold of him. In the meantime, I'll call you when I gather up any identification that will help Dec with his bank account."

I put Charlie's number into my cell, glad that I

had a lead, even if I couldn't get a hold of him right now. I'd keep trying.

"I appreciate your help, Trudy." Standing, I held out my hand for her to shake. She stood and returned the gesture.

"Any friend of Dec's is a friend of mine. I'll be in touch." With that she turned and walked away, leaving me with an uneasy lump in my gut and a million thoughts running through my head.

Scanning the area, I searched for any sign of Harley, but the large grassy park had swallowed him up. Did I wait around or head home? Search for him? He had no transport or money.

Perhaps the walk home would do him good. A ten minute drive would probably equate to an hour's walk or more. If he remembered the route we'd taken.

Taking out the piece of paper with his apartment address on it, I decided to do a detour on the way home.

Chapter Twenty-One

Harley

Wife. Wife. Wife. The word re-ran in my head like a stuck record. *Your father's dead* added to the mix and I could barely focus on putting one foot in front of the other.

What should I be feeling? Grief? I could no longer grieve than I could recall what I did two weeks ago.

Hitting the side of my head, I let my anger surface. I thought finding out about my past would be a good thing, but so far, none of it was thrilling me. My safe bubble with Mac had well and truly burst, and I scrambled to hold onto the remnants.

A wife I had separated from. How did I know she'd been telling the truth about us agreeing to reconcile? It could have been made up in an attempt to win me back. Her perusal of Mac hadn't escaped me. Jealousy appearing for a moment before she'd reined it in.

Shit. Mac. I'd stormed off and left her with

Trudy. She must be reeling from too much information, like me. What would she be thinking? Could she possibly be happy we'd run into Trudy and I may finally be getting the answers I needed?

The idea of losing her scared the hell out of me. To never see her again. Talk to her. Touch her. It would break me. But how did I deal with still being married? And my mother. Should I go visit the woman? Would it destroy her to see me like this?

My life officially sucked. This morning I'd been happily ensconced in my world filled with Mac, and in a split second I felt like I'd stepped into an alternate universe.

Taking pause, I surveyed my surroundings. Gone was the park with the oversized circus tent and in its place stood a part of town as alien as my last name. Houses lined each side of the wide street, and in hindsight it had been a stupid move to walk off when I didn't know how the hell to find my way back to Mac's apartment from my new location.

Shit. What the hell would I do now? I had no cell phone, and even if I did, I didn't know Mac's number.

Remembering the card I'd stuffed in my pocket from Trudy, I pulled it out and stared at it. Should I find a phone and call her collect to come get me? Did I really have any other choice?

Feeling stupid for storming off, I began to walk again, hoping I'd stumble across a gas station or business where I could ask to use their phone. As much as I didn't want to call her, I needed to get back to Mac's apartment. To safety. I was exposed. I'd forgotten all about having a possible target on my back. It had seeped to the shadows after Trudy appeared. If someone wanted me dead, they could take me down right now.

Standing taller and drawing my inner warrior out, I scanned the vicinity, on guard once more. The way I felt, if an attacker approached he would bear the brunt of my wrath. I silently dared them to try.

The sun heated my core as I continued my trek. Thoughts kept switching to Mac. From the moment I first heard her voice in my consciousness, a strange connection had formed. She had a way about her that I likened to a magnet. She wasn't even aware of it, and perhaps I clung to false hope, but being with her felt right. Familiar. Home. Her smile could light up an entire state. Her laugh, a song on its own. Now, while I trekked in the middle of nowhere on my own, I craved to see her hypnotic eyes and to have her invisible charm wrap around me in comfort. But where did Trudy's revelation leave her? Leave us? Were we an *us* or perhaps my gratitude toward her had morphed into some misguided affection? No. My heart told me otherwise.

After another twenty minutes of left and right turns filled with hope, I came across a gas station. Perhaps I'd been going in circles, I couldn't be sure, but the sight had me breathe out in relief.

Dodging incoming cars, I made my way inside to the cashier, waiting in line as he served customers first. With only one guy working the register, the line crawled slowly. Only one person paid in cash, which had all the card purchases extend my waiting time. Finally, I stood before the guy.

"Hey," he chirped.

"Hi. Do you have a payphone I could use? I left my cell at home and need to contact a friend to pick me up." I wasn't about to blurt out the truth and have the two people behind me listen in.

With a nod to the back wall, the pimply faced dude, who only looked to be twenty, if that, didn't utter any more, he merely waited for me to move so he could serve the next person.

Offering him a reciprocal nod in return, I swiveled and followed his vague direction, past some aisles stocked with food to the last row. Finding the payphone in the right-hand corner, I hoped it would allow me to make a collect call.

With Trudy's card still in my hand, I scanned the writing on the front of the large phone, noting the message about dialing '0' to be put through to an operator.

Following the instructions, I awaited Trudy to pick up.

After four rings, she answered. "Hello?"

"Uhh. Hey Trudy. It's Harley."

The long pause had me wonder if she'd connect the name to me. For some reason I couldn't associate myself with Declan. She clicked after a few more beats.

"Dec? Where are you?" Concern laced her words.

"I'm not sure. I walked a fair way from the park and ended up finding a gas station." Embarrassed at the next statement, I took a deep breath. "I don't know how to find my way back."

"I'll come get you. Can you ask the attendant

which gas station you're at? The suburb, maybe?" She didn't hesitate in her offer of help. I sighed with relief.

"That's gonna be a bit hard 'cause I'm calling from a payphone, and the guy is busy serving."

"Can you place the phone down for a moment and ask someone?"

Turning back to face the front, I checked the people waiting in line, pondering on whom would be the best to ask.

"Hang on a sec," I told Trudy, placing the receiver temporarily on the top of the phone.

The nice middle-aged lady at the back of the line looked as good as any person to ask.

"Excuse me?" I tapped her on the arm.

Spinning around and looking up, she raised her eyebrows curiously. "Yes?"

"I'm new in town. Could you please give me the address here? I need a friend to pick me up."

"Oh sure." She rattled off the street name before I thanked her and returned to my awaiting call.

"You still there, Trudy?"

"Yeah, Dec."

I began to think she called me that on purpose to piss me off. She needed to call me by the name I knew. "It's Harley." I gave her the address before she could speak.

I could hear a loud exhale over the line. "Ooookay. *Harley*. I'll be there in ten minutes. Be waiting out front so I can see you."

"Thank you. You're a lifesaver." I meant it. I wasn't sure what I would have done if I didn't have her number.

"That's what wives are for, right?"

I couldn't answer. I didn't know what she had ever done for me. I wasn't comfortable hearing the term from her, and I couldn't be sure as to why.

"See you soon." I hung up and walked out into the fresh air, suddenly feeling like the enclosed space inside suffocated me.

Even the overwhelming stench of gasoline had me breathe easier. I didn't do confined spaces crammed with people. Noted.

Passing numerous makes and models of cars, I wondered what I owned. I made a note to ask Trudy if she knew. Mac's Mustang was dope. I'd enjoy a ride like that. Mac. Thoughts turned to her again. She took up a lot of my headspace. Fate had brought her to me and I planned on keeping her in my life regardless of what memories surfaced of my past. My feelings for her were real. The only real thing I knew. Everything else scared me.

Tiny details of my life eluded me. Would I ever get everything back? Or would it only be pieces? Waking up with no memory was akin to being reborn as an adult. I didn't need to be taught how to eat, dress, shower or use the toilet. They were already hardwired into me. It wasn't *doing* things I had a problem with. I needed to know exactly what had led me to Mac's ICU and why. And Trudy. A niggling seed of doubt had planted itself into my brain about her and I. There had to be more to it than my constant deployment. She had obviously known going into the marriage that I'd be on assignment a lot. No. She hadn't told me everything.

Standing on the curb, I tucked the card I was still gripping into my pocket and waited.

Chapter Twenty-Two

Mac

Slowing down to a crawl, I found the apartment complex Trudy had given me. Turning onto a paved road, I began my search for number twenty five.

The white sided homes with black roofs lined both sides of me like tall hedges in a maze as I turned corner after corner until finally I found it. Tucked at the far side of the estate sat Harley's place.

Parking for a moment out front, knowing I wouldn't be able to stay long, I searched for any sign of the guy who'd been living with me. The porch lay empty, no shoes lined up. Aside from a weary looking garden with a few weeds, I couldn't associate him to the condo. The front window had a blind drawn, so taking a quick peek wasn't an option. Curiosity nipped at my heels to find out more about the man who had managed to burrow under my skin.

The single garage jutting out from the right hand

side had no vehicle out front. If he owned one it would be locked away.

Taking pause to soak in the place he called home, I couldn't help but wonder what secrets were held within its walls. He'd gone about his life not too long ago, not even knowing I existed and vice-versa. It's funny how things had come to pass. What had his thoughts been the last time he lived here? Had he brought other women home after he'd separated from Trudy? What did the place look like inside? Messy or clean? There were so many questions I wanted answers to.

Futile in my attempt to learn anything knew, I backed out and had to remember how to snake my way out to the gate.

A few kids played with a ball on the quiet street leading away from Harley's home, but apart from that, the place appeared deserted.

Upon reaching the gate, I noticed rows of mailboxes on a brick wall which also acted as part of the estate's front entrance. An idea popped into my head as I veered off the street onto the grassy verge.

At least the mailboxes were in order, unlike the condos. Finding number twenty-five proved easy. It overflowed with junk and letters, so I pulled as many as I could out, knowing I'd left some behind that were locked inside.

With my stash in the car, I drove home, hoping when I arrived Harley had returned.

***

The apartment echoed with emptiness, which had me worrying. Should I have gone searching for him? Could he find his way home? Well, to my home. Not his.

Deciding to wait the afternoon out, I put a pot of coffee on and set his mail on the kitchen counter, pondering over whether I should take a peek or not.

I wasn't snoopy by nature, but the white envelopes bundled together were calling to me.

Huffing out a breath, I walked down the hall and pulled my nurse's uniform from the clean laundry pile and began ironing it to give me something to do besides think of a tall, sinful, mysterious male. The husband of Trudy. Ugh. While I didn't want to be the *other woman,* technically while he lived under my roof, I played that role. She seemed to take the news about Harley better than I would have in her situation. She still cared about him. If he regained his memory, would he still care for her, or had too much water passed under the bridge?

Hanging up my uniform in the closet so it wouldn't be creased for the morning, I moved back to the kitchen to make my coffee. My stomach rumbled, but I wasn't hungry now that I'd had time to digest everything that had gone down this morning.

Would Harley come back or would everything prove too much for him? Where would he go, though? With his wife?

Sipping my too hot coffee, feeling the burn but not really registering it, I eyed the mail still sitting in a pile, begging to be looked through.

Rising, I shuffled to the counter and picked up

the letters, leaving the junk mail, and returned to my seat.

Declan Peterson. It ran strangely over my tongue like tasting a foreign food for the first time. Seeing it printed in bold type brought home the real fact that he wasn't Harley. He never would be. He wasn't even Declan Peterson. It was simply an alias.

Turning over the first envelope, I searched for the company that sent it but couldn't find any return sender. Bold black type on the front spelled out the address I'd visited earlier.

The next was from Bank of America. Good to know. If Trudy came through with ID, he'd surely be able to access his bank account.

The next two had only Harley's name and address on them and the last one had a P.O. Box typed at the top of the envelope but no business name.

Not much help at all. Throwing them on the table, I suddenly remembered Charlie's number I'd keyed into my cell.

Fetching it out of my bag, I found his number and dialed, not really knowing what I would say, but doing it before I could chicken out. It rang and rang and went to voice mail. A deep, well-spoken drawl gave the verse that he couldn't take the call, so I left a rather nervous message about me being a friend of Declan Peterson. I'd almost said Harley, but had changed it at the last moment.

Hoping the guy would eventually return my call, I felt I'd done everything I could.

The only thing to do now was wait.

Chapter Twenty-Three

Harley

Fifteen minutes later an azure blue, late model sedan pulled up with a Nissan badge on the front. Whatever Trudy did for a career must have her living comfortably. Stopping in front of me, she opened her door and appeared over the roof with one leg still in the car.

"Hey…er…Harley. Sorry it took a while. Traffic's a nightmare." With her eyes she motioned for me to get in.

Grateful for her appearance, I smiled and walked around to the passenger side and climbed in.

"I appreciate you coming to get me. I didn't have anyone else to call."

Raising her right brow slightly she slanted me a look. "Mac not give you her cell number?"

I didn't have it hardwired into my brain. There had been no need to call her since being released from hospital. And besides, we'd been together the whole time. "If I had my cell, I would have keyed in her number, but I don't have a thing. Even the clothes on my back are borrowed."

Frowning, she turned to face the front, peering out the windscreen. "It must be tough for you. Waking up a stranger, even to yourself. Did the doctors say when you'd get your full memory back?"

The hitch in her voice didn't go unnoticed, and I quickly grasped the hidden meaning in her question. Would I remember our life together? Would I want to pick up where we'd left things?

The truth of it was, I didn't know anymore. Everything had changed. Perhaps, I'd changed. Mac had manifested out of thin air into my life, and if things went back to normal, where would it leave my feelings for her?

Buckling my belt, I replied. "They couldn't be certain. I may regain it all, or I may have pieces I never remember."

Nodding, she rolled us away from the curb and into bustling traffic.

"Where to? Did you want to stop by your apartment? You obviously won't have a key, but maybe it will spark something in your mind."

My apartment. Rolling it around my head a few times, I sought an image of what it looked like but I came up blank. Maybe I should listen to Trudy. Seeing it again might trigger something. So far, I had nothing that I'd owned previously. Everything had been borrowed. To know I owned the apartment brought a small amount of comfort.

"Sure."

I didn't know what else to say. My wife sat

beside me, a stranger, so even trivial conversation eluded me. She remained quiet too, perhaps knowing I wouldn't be able to answer most questions or relate to anything we used to share. Awkward tension filled the small space. I felt like she needed me to say something but I wasn't sure what.

Making our way through the center of town again and seeing the circus tent, thoughts turned to Mac again. I needed to ask something.

"Uh, is Mac okay? Did she go home?"

Keeping my eyes focused straight ahead, I could see out of my peripheral vision when Trudy turned to look at me for a brief moment.

Taking in a deep breath, she said, "She's as confused as I am. Concerned about you and wanting answers. I'm not sure where she went." Her voice sounded off as she finished the last sentence and I wondered what she thought of my relationship with Mac.

"She seems like a nice girl." Trudy made Angel seem like a teenager. She certainly wasn't one. But then, my ex-wife didn't know Mac like I did, and even though we were only separated by age a few years, Trudy make it sound like I had snatched from the cradle.

Still, it must be hard for her. If the situation were reversed, I doubt I'd be handling it as well.

"She is. She helped me immensely when I woke with no memory." What more could I say? That I had feelings for my nurse? Somehow, I doubted those words would go down well.

"So...are you two, you know...dating?" We

turned off the main road and into a quieter area. I should have been paying attention to where we were going, but my mind became occupied with all things Mac.

"No. She helped me out and I've been helping her out by staying. Her boyfriend took off and then we came home to her apartment, completely trashed. I think she feels safer with me there." Trudy didn't need to know we'd groped each other before coming to our senses. She didn't need to know how Mac anchored me. Someone I clung to in my suspended reality. Someone I had gotten to know as Harley and not Declan.

As I glanced sideways, I caught Trudy's shoulders relaxing slightly at my answer.

Slowing down, I focused out her window as we turned into a set of condominiums.

"This where I lived?"

"Yeah. You recognize it?"

"Not yet." I blew out a frustrated breath. How could I not even remember where I'd lived for Christ's sake? Nothing about the place sparked familiarity.

Trudy turned into a driveway. A large number twenty five positioned itself on the front door.

I sat and stared at my home, wondering what I lived like. My furnishings and personal items. Clothing. What food remained in my refrigerator? Stupid trivial things I wanted to know.

Feeling a hand on my arm, she asked quietly, "You okay?"

Nodding, I pulled away, exiting her car and striding to the front door. Of course it remained locked up, but that didn't stop me from trying the handle. A small window at the left hand side had a blind drawn, so I couldn't see in. The notion I'd absent-mindedly left a window unlocked sounded crazy, but I had to try. Inside sat my life. Answers. Hopefully even some cash I could use. Ignoring Trudy, who remained in the car with the engine running, obviously not planning on me being more than a couple of minutes, I gave the garage door a shake, but it didn't budge.

There had to be a way out back. I crept closer to finding out some truths and yet, I couldn't find a way into my own damn home. Did I need to smash a window?

Identical condos butted against mine on either side with no gates in between. Jesus. Gripping my neck hard, I spun back around and found Trudy with her door open, engine off. She eyed me as if I might detonate like a bomb. One truth remained firmly. She knew the real me, even when I didn't.

"Is there an onsite manger?" I asked, grabbing at straws. Someone had to have a master key, surely.

"Ah, no, Dec. I'm, pretty sure you bought the place. Only you have a key."

Hearing my alter ego this time snapped something inside of me. Moving closer to her, I slammed my hand down on the roof of her car. "It's Harley! I've told you not to call me Dec or Declan! I don't know that guy! He means nothing to me! I can't be someone I'm not. I may never be him. Ever."

She appeared shell-shocked and shrank back into the car. Her lip quivered, softening me only a little as I turned and began pacing. I needed Mac. I needed to hear her voice. Her song. Anything. She calmed me when I felt like drowning.

"Take me to Mac's," I demanded, stalking to the passenger side and getting in.

Without a sound, Trudy turned the key and reversed before driving off.

"Do you know how to get there?" She spoke so quietly, I had to strain to hear it properly.

"I know my way back from the circus tent. Return there and I think I'll be able to find her place."

I suddenly felt shitty for taking my anger out on Trudy. She didn't ask for any of this. She'd been caught up in the middle of it without a choice.

"I'm sorry for getting annoyed with you. I guess everything is finally taking its toll. I just need some time to process it."

"I know. You have my number…if you need to ask anything or talk." I could have sworn she sniffled on the verge of tears, so I didn't add to the conversation.

Upon reaching the circus tent, familiarity began to wash over me. "Turn left up ahead." I signaled, glad I'd taken notice of the drive into town from Macs.

The clock on the dash read three p.m. The time had zipped by. I hadn't eaten lunch and needed food. Directing Trudy to Mac's apartment, I twisted in my seat as we stopped. "Thank you. I mean it. I don't know what I would have done if you hadn't given me your number. I realize how hard this must be for you, and I'm sorry." I meant every word.

She smiled for the first time in a while. "Glad I could help. Take care, Harley."

Returning her smile, glad she hadn't called me Dec, I got out and moved toward Mac's front door, wondering what reception I would be met with.

Chapter Twenty-Four

Mac

A car rolled into my short driveway at the front of the single car garage, not idling for long before disappearing.

Instinct told me Harley had come home, but I couldn't be sure until he opened the door and confirmed my suspicions. I sat on the sofa, reading a novel I'd had on the *to be read* pile on my Kindle for months. I'd perused the same paragraph about thirty times, seeing the words but not absorbing them.

Harley had taken up way too much of my mind space. Not only did I worry about him, I had changed my mind a few times about whether I should let him keep staying with me or not. The quandary had me all kinds of knotted up.

He gingerly stepped through the door, eyes fixed on me, not quite a smile on his face. "Hey."

"Hey." Placing my Kindle on the coffee table, I asked, knowing full well the answer to the question but wanting him to confirm it, "Did you find your way home okay?"

"Trudy gave me a lift."

Bingo. "Oh. Well, where did you go after you left the park?"

He moved slowly forward. Tentatively. Still watching me. His eyes were black marbles.

"I needed to clear my head. I took a walk."

"And you ran into Trudy again?" Did the tone of my voice sound slightly jealous?

"No. I…uh…kind of got lost."

"So you called her." Okay, that tone sounded a lot like jealousy.

"I didn't have your number. She gave me her card."

He came close enough to touch. From this height, I was eye level with his sturdy thighs. If I raised my sights a little higher…

No. Focus, Mac. Trudy, remember?

The sensible side of my brain took over. The side that quickly analyzed situations at work in the blink of an eye and acted accordingly.

On a full inhale, I let my breath out and began. "Harley. Dec. Whatever your name is. You'd better sit." I motioned beside me without catching his expression. If I found his emotive eyes, I'd cave and throw myself at him rather than do the right thing. Sometimes it sucked to have a conscience.

Cautiously he sat, his leg an inch from mine. His mere presence fluttered my stomach and chest.

"Mac…"

"No, let me say what I have to. Please."

When he made no effort to proceed, I swallowed

my urge to reach out to him and filled the silence. "I've been doing some thinking of my own while you've been out. I know you don't remember much about life with Trudy, but I think the best thing for you to do would be to forget about me and focus on her. Your wife. See if it triggers your memory. She's the only link to your past. Over time, it's bound to help you remember. As long as you're with me, I don't think it's going to happen. You have your own apartment now."

My face remained as stoic as I could make it, even though my heart bled. I could hear him breathing beside me.

I heard one of his knuckles crack. "What if I don't want to remember? What if I don't want that life? What if I want to pursue whatever this thing is between us?"

A large hand moved to caress the back of my head, pulling my hair away from my neck.

Contact had me shivering and unable to form a sentence, but I couldn't let his physical effect on me deter me from doing the right thing.

"I know you think you feel something for me, but I'm sure it's a case of gratitude. You're grateful for me being the only one there. For helping you." Finally I gained the courage to turn my head and raise my eyes north and gaze into his. Pain and sadness etched into the lines on his brow and the reflection in his gaze.

His hand moved around to cup my jaw, his thumb brushing over my lips. "You think this is gratitude?"

Using all my strength, I ignored the sensation the

pad of his thumb elicited on my mouth. "Your emotions are all over the place right now. Nothing is as it seems. I don't know the real you."

His eyes squinted half shut. "Are you serious? Angel, you may not know the life I lived, but me being here with you and touching you *is* the real me. What I feel when you're near is not fake. Don't you get that?"

The beginnings of a tear formed in the corner of my eye, but I held it at bay. I'd longed to hear that his feelings were real, and yet at the same time, it confused me.

For the first time in my life, a man I truly felt I could fall hard for told me what I wanted to hear. What I hoped to hear. A man who would treat me like a queen if I let him. But I needed to be selfless and give him the space and time to piece together his shattered life. My being in the middle would only hinder that. We'd spent so much time together since he awoke, there hadn't been any true separation to allow for objectivity.

Placing my hand over his, I gently drew his fingers away, swallowing hard. "Look. I'll be honest when I say there is definitely an attraction there on my behalf, and you seem sincere when you say you feel it too, but what sort of a person would I be if I didn't take a step back and give you time to amass what you once had? You have a mother and friends who will want to see you. A wife who you were working things out with. I don't think I could sleep at night knowing I took you away from all that."

His jaw hardened and the light began fading

from his eyes. "So you really do want me to move out? What about the danger you could be in? I'm not leaving here until you get a damn security alarm installed." His voice rose. I didn't want an argument.

"Fine. While I'm at work tomorrow, call someone and have them come out and take a look. I'll do a search later and write down a couple of numbers."

The tension I'd felt rolling off him at the park this morning resumed. Knowing I played a small part, I attempted to appease him.

"I'm sorry, Harley. I know you've had a shit day, and my asking you to move out has added to it, but you need to see things from my perspective."

"Your perspective? What about my perspective? You're all I have. All I recognize." He stood and walked into the kitchen, leaving me with a high level of guilt.

Moving off the sofa and following, I found him downing a large glass of water, his back to me.

Defending my actions, I stopped in the doorway. "I never should have let things get this far. I blame myself."

His broad back rose and fell as he placed the empty glass in the sink. Turning to face me, the sad expression had me almost run to him to take back everything I had said.

"So that's it? You're leaving me to deal with this alone?"

"No! I'll still be here for you as a friend. I promised I'd help you."

God. I didn't want to be *just* friends. My body

didn't want it, and my heart didn't want it. My brain led the race though. Doing the right thing had always been in my nature.

He closed his eyes and sucked in air deeply though his nose. "If that's what you've chosen, then I guess I don't have a choice."

Suddenly remembering Harley's mail on the counter, I grabbed it and held it out for him. "Here. I did a drive by of your apartment today. I don't know what I hoped to find. A clue, perhaps. This mail stuck out of the box. I brought it here for you. I thought there may be something important."

His stare penetrated mine for a moment too long before he strode forward and almost snatched it from me.

"Thank you." He huffed, sitting at the table, opening the first envelope.

Deciding to leave him to it, I walked into the bathroom and turned on the shower, needing some hot water to help me settle. What had I just done? Had I pushed him away for good?

Chapter Twenty-Five

Harley

The idea of leaving Mac had me tied up in all sorts of tight knots. Little Miss Righteous had played her 'do good' card and it pissed me off. I couldn't merely step back into my old world and pretend as if things were back to normal. Nothing would ever be that way. She seemed to dismiss the chemistry between us so easily, as if it meant nothing to her.

Hearing the water switch off in the shower, I waited for her to return to the living room while I finished browsing through my mail. Nothing worth keeping except a bank statement. Good to find. My account number had been typed at the top, so tomorrow I'd contact them. Noting the name Declan Peterson threw me another curve ball. Just who in the hell was I? Just another question I needed answers to. Why didn't I carry my father's last name? I couldn't process anymore, so instead I threw a question at Mac.

"Do you have a Swiss army knife?"

She spun to my voice in alarm. "Why?"

"If it's not too much trouble, I'd like to break into my own apartment. Grab some clothes and take a look around. See if I have any ID. If I'm moving out, I need to get a new key cut too."

"Oh, sure. Give me a minute to grab some shoes and we'll head over. I don't have an army knife, but I have a hairpin. Will that do?"

Her tentative reply told me she hadn't expected me to suggest returning to my home so soon, even to simply snoop. "We'll soon find out."

Shuffling away, I watched her shoulders slump. Damn woman. Why did she fight her attraction to me? We only had the present moment, so why not live in it?

Fifteen minutes later we stood outside my front door, me needing to siphon in deep, calming breaths as I geared myself to step over the threshold into a life I knew nothing about. Mac stayed close, thankfully. I couldn't do it on my own.

Inserting the hairpin into the lock, I jiggled it around as if I'd done it a thousand times, listening for the telltale click before slowly pushing the door open.

"Do you want me to go in first?" Mac asked.

"No. I got this. Just stay near me."

She didn't respond as I crossed over the line into a small, dark kitchen. I drew the blinds to let in some natural light. A couple of dishes sat in the sink, but overall it looked pretty clean and tidy. Glancing around, I searched for things I might recognize, spotting a photo on the white refrigerator door. Moving closer, I could see Trudy and me, obviously in happier times. We were on a beach, arms wrapped around each other, smiling genuinely into the camera. My dream came back to me and I wondered if the location were one and the same. Honeymoon perhaps? Placing the magnet back on the photo, I turned, eying Mac as she stared at the picture before looking away and down to the floor.

I squeezed her shoulder as I moved past into an open plan living area. Beige couch with lighter colored walls and carpet had the place looking homely. A magazine lay open on a timber coffee table with an empty mug beside it. A large flat screen television hung from a bracket on the left wall, but apart from that, there were minimal furnishings. Nothing feminine about it at all. A typical bachelor pad.

The musty smell had me opening some windows to let in the fresh breeze.

"I'm gonna go pack a bag and search around for some identification. You want to make a coffee or something?" I asked, watching Mac fidget nervously. "Actually, I'm not sure what's in the cupboard, but feel free to have a look."

She offered me a tight smile and a slight nod, so I left her to it. I was anxious to see more.

There were two bedrooms, a spare and the master suite, which had been done out in similar tones as the rest of the apartment. A small bathroom sat between each bedroom down the hallway.

The main bedroom is what drew me. My room. Standing in it brought forward the weirdest sensation. I paused, surrounded by pieces of myself

I knew nothing about. A book sat on the nightstand, marked at the page I'd been reading. *Game of Thrones.* Wow! I never would have guessed. I'd had no interest to pick up a book since awakening. Perhaps because Mac had been my sole focus.

Stepping into the closet, I pored over my clothes. Jeans, t-shirts, a couple of black suits. Leather jackets. It formed a picture in my mind about my tastes. Running shoes and black military style boots sat, neatly on the floor. A laundry hamper sat in a corner and the clothes hanging over the edge caught my eye. Camouflage gear. Definitely military. Picking up the shirt, I brought it to my nose, inhaling the fabric which still had remnants of sweat around the armpits. A flash came to me. Sudden and fierce.

"What are you reading, Reno?" Viper asked, swigging water from his flask as we sat in the army helicopter waiting to take off to our classified location somewhere in the Afghan mountains.

We were fitted out in our full military gear, ready to fight. The rundown had been rebel soldiers had overtaken a tiny mountainous settlement. There had already been bloodshed. We were heading in to end it and to retrieve any survivors.

Viper sat beside me. Reno opposite, poring over a letter like his life depended on it. Six other troops were settling into their seats, belting up.

"Mind your own business, asshole." He always joked with Viper. All the guys cussed and ribbed each other, especially right before a mission. It helped to keep things light, as if we weren't about to

be dropped into the middle of a war zone.

"Oooh. Reno's got a girl. Who is she, Nevada? Some stripper from all the clubs you frequent? You finally been whipped by one?" Viper jeered, placing his water into the pocket of his backpack.

"Fuck you! This ain't no stripper. She's someone special." Reno's eyes fluttered to me but didn't linger, his cheeks pinking. His fingers shook as he creased the page, folding it up and putting it back in its envelope and then into his top pocket like some good luck charm.

He didn't normally show fear before battle, but as he sat there avoiding everyone's eyes, he appeared rattled.

"You okay, man?" I asked, wondering if something in the letter had changed his mood.

Closing his eyes, leaning his head back against the fuselage of the chopper, he nodded. "Just got too much adrenalin pouring through my veins, that's all."

That better be it, because the team couldn't afford to have him off his game.

The whir of the rotor started and we were soon airborne.

"Harley?"

I spun fast, squeezing the shirt I still held, letting the dregs of my memory slip away.

"You all right? What are you doing?" Mac looked to the shirt and then up at me.

Tossing the item of clothing back in the hamper, I faked a smile. "I think I remembered something. Just a memory of Reno."

"Oh? You want to talk about it?"

"Nah. It's nothing important."

Mac appeared disappointed.

"If it's anything I deem important, I'll keep you updated, don't worry." Pushing past her, I scoured the bedroom for any identification or money.

Rummaging through a timber set of drawers beside the large, black sleigh bed, I pulled out some boxers and threw them on the bed.

"Can you check back in the closet for an overnight bag?" I asked Mac, while I continued to dig.

"Sure." She padded off, leaving me to my own thoughts.

The bottom drawer housed some neatly folded shorts, so I pulled a couple of pairs out and tossed them with the boxers. Nothing other than clothes nestled inside the bureau.

Noticing one on the other side, I crawled across the white sheets, which had been neatly made, hospital tucks at each corner. Definitely military.

Spying something of significance atop the drawers, I picked them up, instantly knowing what they were. My black dog tags. A voice within told me this could be a significant break into finding out my true identity.

"Mac?"

"Yeah?" she called from the closet.

"I think I've found something."

Turning to watch her, she exited with a black overnight back and placed it on the bed before walking around to me and sitting on the edge.

"This is awesome! Can I see?" She held out her

delicate hand, so I placed the black metal in it. "It has your last name, social security number, and birth date on here."

"Do you think the bank will let me access my accounts with these?"

"Let's just keep searching first. See what else we can find. I'm pretty sure you'll need photo ID."

Handing me the dog tags, I put them in my pocket and searched the second set of drawers.

A tatty copy of James Patterson's *Along Came a Spider* sat atop a few envelopes, so I lifted them out and began opening each one.

Mac had moved into the kitchen. Cupboards opened and closed, cutlery clinking. There must be something else we could find.

One of the letters opened was a receipt for a vehicle. My vehicle. I hadn't ventured into the garage yet. A 2012 model Ford F-150. Color, black. Intriguing. But first I needed to search these other letters.

Finding nothing but old invoices and receipts, I closed the drawer and made my way out to Mac.

"Find anything else?" I asked, watching her shirt ride up as she stretched to a high cupboard above the stove.

"No. You?"

"Nothing but a vehicle receipt. I grinned. "I'm heading out to the garage to check my pickup."

"You have a truck?"

"Going by a receipt I found. Yep."

Before I took a step, her cell pealed out of her purse, which sat on the counter. Glancing at me, she dug it out and answered. "Hello?"

Deciding not to eavesdrop, I stalked to the garage, still being able to hear the one sided conversation.

"Good. We're at his apartment now. You did? Great, we'll come and pick it up."

Silence.

"Oh. Okay. I'll let him know. See you soon."

Intrigue left me the moment I found the shiny black truck in front of me. Fat tires made her appear beefy. The chrome on her front grill sparkled to perfection. I'd taken pride in my stuff.

Opening the driver's door, I climbed in and sat behind the wheel, getting a feel for her. The interior was also black and as clean as a whistle. The glove compartment beckoned me. If there were any documents I needed to keep pertaining to the vehicle, they would be in there.

A flashlight sat beside a travel pack of tissues, and underneath lay a driver's manual along with a registration document. Bingo. Another form of ID I may be able to use. Folding it back up, I scanned the rest of the interior, not finding anything else.

Mac appeared at the door leading from the garage into the living room.

"Trudy called."

"What did she want, and how did she have your number?"

"We swapped numbers at the park. She's on her way over with a copy of your marriage certificate."

I wasn't sure how to react to that. Another great form of identification, but it also confirmed the vows I'd taken with a woman I knew nothing about. Having real proof frightened me.

Blowing out a breath, I combed my hair with my fingers. "Okay. I guess that's good, right?"

Mac appeared crestfallen, but the strong woman in her attempted to hide it by plastering a fake smile on her face. "It's great you're finally getting pieces of the puzzle put together."

Needing to touch her and appease her doubts, I stood before her in three strides. This close, I could hear her rapid breathing and sharp intake of breath.

"Angel?" I asked, hoping to draw her face up to mine.

As if unable to fight our combined static electricity, slowly her chin lifted and I peered into her magnificent eyes.

"Mmm?"

"You and me. This thing between us. I'm not gonna lose it. We'll find a way to sort all the shit out and then I'm coming for you."

She blinked twice and chewed the inside of her cheek. "You need to give Trudy a chance."

Shuffling my feet, urging her backwards, I forced her back into the wall, leaning over her with my elbow above her head. "I don't want Trudy. I want you. Even if I remember every damn thing I've ever done since birth, I'll still want you." I lowered my head, not touching her in any way, but filling her with my heat, showing her how much I meant every word.

"You feel that, Angel?"

She could only nod, while locked onto my laser-like attention.

"Yeah. That's what I'm talking about. You fill me up when you're near, like a sweet elixir I need just to survive. It drives me crazy."

Unable to maintain my *no contact* policy, I gripped her chin with my thumb and forefinger, holding her in place. Not that she could move with me all but plastered to her. My chest heaved, my heart absorbing her essence into every chamber.

"Give me the word. I want to taste that sweet mouth of yours. Jesus, woman. Don't deprive me of that. It's the only real thing I've got."

My restraint dwindled fast as she dithered, fighting with her willpower. Her eyes glazed over. She could no more refrain from me than I could from her. The imperceptible assent of her head, the only invite I needed. Finally.

I drove my mouth forward like the starving beast she made me. Sweet heaven, the immediate relief scratched an itch. It would suffice for the time being, but without a doubt the itch would return stronger than ever.

I groaned into her mouth when her tongue licked mine, pressing my body tightly against hers, needing more than I knew she would give me, but relishing in it all the same. Our lips sealed together perfectly with just the right amount of pressure. Moving my hand from her chin to her choppy hair, I grasped her scalp, pulling her forward even further, unable to get enough.

Her mews spurred me on harder, my body officially leading the race. My head filled with the sensation of Mac. Nothing else.

"Lift your leg."

She complied, giving me the leverage to hoist her up around my waist. Never breaking contact from her devastating lips, I spun and sat her on the hood of my pickup. It felt animalistic. My hands took on a life of their own, moving furiously as I ground into her. She nipped at my lower lip, sounds erupting from her throat when I hit the spot she needed me most.

Both her hands cupped my ass as she perched on the edge of my hood, her ankles crossed at my lower back.

Everything in me quieted in her presence. Her ability to erase my anxiety gave me the balm I needed to simply exist. I needed that. I needed her.

"Harley…" she whimpered, her head floppy as she angled it to the side, offering me the elegant column to suck and lick.

An inferno of desire burned my loins, threatening to turn me to ash. I bit into her neck teasingly, and then soothed it with a large swipe of my tongue. She cried out. Desperate.

Groping underneath her shirt, I found my target and gloved her ample breasts, squeezing and kneading in between flicking her rock hard capsules.

"Yessss. That feels amazing," she crooned, her head thrusting back.

So far she hadn't pushed me away, so I let my hands feather down her sides to her jeans, where I found the button and popped it open. Still she let me continue.

"So beautiful," I admired. A goddess. Without a doubt. Her flat stomach led to a fully waxed opening between her legs that had me sucking in air sharply. My head dropped to watch as I pushed her jeans and white lace panties down in one swoop. The sight of her bare before me nearly had me detonate there and then, but I held it together by a thread, not wanting to appear like a horny teen with no self-control.

A hand slid down and nestled between her legs, cupping her first and then sliding backwards and forwards on her slick folds. She shuddered on the brink, and I knew it wouldn't take much to finish her off.

"Does it feel good, having me adore you like this?" I ground out.

"God, yes. I can't hold on much longer. It's been so long…" She cut herself off, perhaps not wanting to remind either of us about her dry spell. A gorgeous woman had needs and deserved to be taken care of. I offered her that. Right here. Right now.

"Fuck, Angel. Invite me in. Now." The anticipation of penetrating her silky channel with my fingers was killing me.

"Harley. Do it!" she begged, both hands moving from my butt up to my arms so she could cling on.

Two fingers plunged inside, putting her out of her misery. It only served to extend mine, though.

She scalded my fingers. Her walls clung to me, the lightest of flutters giving away her impending release.

"Pull your shirt up so I can suck on those sexy tits." I don't even know where that came from, but I wasn't caring about manners anymore. My jeans were a hindrance and barely holding me together but I needed to take care of Mac first.

Eager to obey, she pulled her shirt and bra up with one hand, exposing two delicacies.

I moaned as I zeroed in on my target. Her chest thrust out, enabling me quite a mouthful. When my lips connected she hissed, followed by a deep, drawn out wail.

I wanted to set her off like a firecracker. Instinct had me curling my two fingers up in a *come hither* motion. That did the trick. A small quiver turned into a rocketing blast of spasms around my fingers.

Her whole body shook. I left her breast to watch her face tighten into a mask of ecstasy. Mouth open, head jerking. The cries that tore from her were almost painful sounding, like she was suffering agony instead of pleasure. I soared with her, keeping my fingers deeply entrenched until I'd wrung every morsel of gratification out of her.

Whispering in her ear, I said, "That's only a snippet of what I want to do to you. I need you on my bed, naked."

A voice startled both of us and popped our bubble. "Oh shit! I'm so sorry. I'll just wait out here."

Mac jumped and instinctively pushed her top down. I dragged my fingers free, pivoting my head around to find Trudy standing in the doorway, cheeks red, hand at her throat. I attempted to shield Mac, but it proved futile. Trudy had obviously seen way more than she should have.

Dragging my fingers slowly out of Mac, disappointment causing me to snap, I barked, "Wait for us in the living room."

When she spun on her heels and disappeared, I

lifted my fingers to my mouth, licking them while searching her face. Our connection had been broken at the interruption, her body stiffening.

Even as her wide eyes latched onto my tongue swiping away her juices, I knew I'd lost her again.

She pushed me away and stood, pulling up her panties and jeans, making sure her clothes were back in place. God, she looked a sight with flushed cheeks and enlarged pupils. Damn Trudy for coming over. I'd become so tightly coiled, needing my own release I teetered on the edge of charging out and raging at her.

"This isn't finished. Not by a long shot," I threw at Mac before turning on my heels and going to greet my wife.

Chapter Twenty-Six

Mac

Mortified didn't accurately describe how I felt. My body had betrayed me and Trudy had walked in on us. She'd probably heard my cries of bliss. What must she think and how could I face her now?

Before I stepped into the kitchen, I listened to Harley's heated voice.

"Jesus, Trudy. Ever hear of knocking?"

"I did knock! I called out but no one answered, so I tried the door and found it unlocked. I searched the whole apartment before hearing noises in the garage. I…uh…I'm sorry I walked in on you."

A breath huffed out. Harley's. "Look, I appreciate you dropping this off. I'm struggling with knowing what to think or feel. I can't pretend like I know you, Trudy. Christ, I'm still trying to decide if I want to visit my own mother!"

"She'll understand if you tell her what happened."

Making an appearance, I stepped into the living

room. Both heads turned to me.

"Coffee?" I squeaked, not knowing what else to ask, but desperately needing a caffeine hit. My embarrassment followed me into the kitchen as I heard both Harley and Trudy answer *yes*.

Keep busy, Mac. Don't lose it.

I made a mistake. A silly, beautiful mistake. I couldn't let it happen again. The sooner Harley moved back into his own place, the better. After tomorrow when my alarm got fitted, he could begin getting his life back. Without me.

After the coffee brewed, the three of us sat in an uneasy silence, until I piped up. It had to be done.

"So. My opinion about keeping some distance from you both still stands. Trudy, Harley's moving back in here tomorrow so he can pick some of his life up."

Two sets of eyes on me were grilling. Especially Harley's. I avoided looking at him until he let loose.

"Jesus, Mac. Are you still set on me living back here? I can't access my bank accounts yet. How am I supposed to survive? After what just happened…"

He didn't finish because Trudy interrupted. "You can stay with me. You know, until we get your money situation sorted."

How convenient, I thought. She jumped right in there, probably waiting for the moment. Why did the idea of them living together turn my stomach? As much as I wanted to step back, I didn't like the thought of them living under the same roof. God, I'd morphed into a hypocrite.

Harley gave her a look that screamed, *are you serious?* And then pinned me with one that set my skin alight. His dusky eyes bored into me with such intensity I had to look down. He hadn't finished his argument with me.

"Not to mention, Angel. Your apartment was broken into, in case you forgot. How can I protect you from here?"

"Once my alarm gets fitted you won't have to," I rebutted.

"What about the times you're not at the apartment?" He rose and took a step toward me and I put my hand up to stop him so I could think straight.

"I can't live in fear. It may have been a random, one-time thing. Criminals searching for drug money?" I didn't really believe that, but I could give him nothing else. Picking up my mug from the small table beside the chair, I took a large swig, letting the taste comfort me and steeling me for what I needed to add. "I think Trudy's right. You should move in with her."

His neck reddened and he balled his fists as his side. Definitely angry. "Fuck, Mac! Are you crazy? I've already led danger to you. Do you want me to lead it to Trudy as well?"

He had a point, but if we were being watched right now, that theory went out the window.

She chimed in, "I have an alarm fitted and live in a safe complex with security. It's probably your best bet until the guy who shot you is caught. Don't you think?"

Harley flung his head back and let out a groan, the arteries in his neck engorged. I hated to agree with Trudy, but she had a good argument. In his apartment he would be vulnerable to an attack.

"Besides," Trudy went on, "I think we had an old joint bank account which still has some funds in it. I don't know why I didn't think of it earlier. It may not be much, but every little bit will help."

Why did she have to be so practical? Maybe that's why Harley had married her, besides her obvious beauty. I imagined her taking care of everything while he dove into his missions and tours. A good little wife.

Downing the rest of my coffee in three gulps, I silently wished vodka would appear so I could wallow in it. Already knowing Harley's answer, I steeled myself.

"Fine. But it won't be for long. Just until I figure things out. It doesn't mean we're back together. And it won't be until after Mac's alarm is fitted." He shot Trudy a warning glare.

She nodded but had a smile plastered on her face. I felt like throwing my empty cup at her head, but I needed to be civil for Harley's sake. "Okay, that's settled. Now, I have to go and pick up some things from the store. I'll leave you two in peace." Her cheeks pinked and I knew she was recalling that dreaded moment when I'd been half-naked.

We didn't walk her to the door. She found her way out. Once her car drove off, Harley approached me. "Why do you want me out so badly?"

He overtook my personal space again as if doing so might intimidate me, but I held my ground. "It's not that. I'm attempting to help you. You just can't see it."

"All I see is a beautifully, stubborn woman who

can't see what's right in front of her. Look at me, Angel. Front and center."

Sighing, I obeyed and absorbed the encompassing male energy he exuded. His ripe mouth glistened and his eyes were nothing short of sinful. Hellfire. What had I been going to say? My mind shut down in a millisecond. Were we now going to finish what we started earlier? I could feel some fierce testosterone breach my comfort zone. He patiently waited for a response, so I blurted out, "I don't want you to go. Not at all." What then? Did I even know? Maybe I ran scared because the man in front of me had me feeling things I never could have dreamed of.

His pointer finger lashed across my lips, backwards and forwards, backwards and forwards.

My insides were a horrendous accumulation of knotted nerves. I wasn't game to blink.

"Then what are you doing, sending me to live with Trudy?" He feathered my cheek.

"You'll be safe there."

"And you won't."

We were going round and round in circles. Stepping out of his trajectory, I moved to the couch, where I plonked down and changed the subject.

"Tomorrow while I'm at work, you need to call the police and see if they have any leads as to who shot you. Surely the cops have a clue by now, if they're doing their job properly."

"It's not black and white like that, Mac. If it's connected with the military, the police might be clueless."

I hadn't thought of that. I'd never lived in a

world which involved criminals and attempted murder. Somehow my life had stepped across the threshold of normal into something else entirely.

"I'll be fine. It's you they're after, not me. I'm just a nurse with no life. What could they possibly want with me?"

Harley sat on the coffee table, facing me. "Leverage."

I let the word ring in my head for a few heartbeats. Could it be possible? I would have thought Trudy would be a better target. Not that I wanted her in mortal danger, but it made more sense.

"I'll keep my trips outside of the hospital to a minimum, if it will make you feel any better. It's not like I had a life before you came along." Immediately I regretted my words. His lips compressed and his pupils enlarged.

He hung his head and shook it. "If I'd known the trouble I'd bring to you, I never would have agreed to come home with you."

I'd insisted. Now I would live with the consequences, whatever they may be.

"If you had your memory, we wouldn't be sitting here having this conversation."

Truth be told, I made the right decision in bringing him home, even if he carried a mountain of baggage. I'd been looking for excitement and fire, and I'd certainly found it.

The million dollar question, though? How would I cope going back to mundane and routine?

Chapter Twenty-Seven

Mac

Work offered a welcome reprieve and left me little time to contemplate anything other than doing rounds and tending to patients.

The accident victim who had taken Harley's place awoke with his full faculties, thankfully. He had been moved to a general ward for recovery.

Char caught up with me in the staff cafeteria at lunch time, eager to learn about my new housemate.

"So, how's our John Doe doing?" Her eyes twinkled and the grin stretched her face wide.

Pouring a coffee, I shucked off my shoes and sat at an empty table. We had the room to ourselves so I was able to talk.

"Ugh, Char, where do I begin? So much has happened since Friday." Waiting for her to fill her cup and join me, I began. "My apartment got trashed on Saturday."

"What? Oh shit, Mac! That's terrible. Are you okay? Did they take anything?"

"Nothing appears to be missing. They did a good job of upending the place, though. If Harley hadn't been there…"

"So they broke in and stole nothing?" Disbelief marred her features.

"I know. I'm surprised too, but I'm certain it's connected to Harley's past."

"Jesus, girl. What have you got yourself into?"

"There's more."

She downed some of her coffee, shaking her head. "I'm not sure I want to know after hearing that."

"Oh, it gets better. We went into town to the festival and who should we run into but his ex-wife? She recognized him, but of course, he didn't have a clue who she was. Turns out they had separated but were in discussions about working everything out."

Char's eyes grew exponentially. "He's married? Wow. How do you feel about that?"

Fingering the handle on my cup, I slanted her a quick eye roll, then peered down at my cup again. "Honestly, I don't have any right to feel anything." I took a deep breath and then blurted out, "But we kissed and sparks flew big time. I'm talking scorching. And now I'm so confused because I want him to stay but I told him he needs to move in with his wife."

I gritted my teeth at the last declaration because it sounded idiotic.

When my friend didn't answer, I peeked up. Her mouth had opened as if to speak but she appeared at a loss for words. I couldn't blame her. I waited. And waited.

"Have I totally lost the plot?" I asked.

Finally she spoke. "Hell, girl. You don't do anything by halves. I can't believe all this has gone on over the span of two days. It's better than a daytime soap."

I needed her to give me advice. Something to help me deal with it. "As my friend, do you have any suggestions?"

"First of all, why in God's name would you send him back to his wife when they'd separated? This is one of the hottest guys to ever grace this medical establishment. Do you need me to slap some sense into you?"

I giggled at her rebuttal. Charlotte and I thought differently when it came to men. If she became attracted to one, nothing else mattered. I, on the other hand, had a conscience.

"It's only until the guy who attacked him is caught."

"That might take years! By then they'll have ten babies! Oh girl, I need to teach you a lesson in catching a man and keeping him."

Coughing on my coffee as I swallowed, I spluttered out, "Nick will be home in a few days."

"And? What's your point? You kick his distant ass to the curb and zero in on the herculean package who clearly wants you."

Heat burned my neck and my eyes shot backwards and forwards nervously.

"You're keeping something else from me. What is it?"

"What?"

"Don't what me! You're doing that thing with your eyes when I know there's something else you haven't told me. Now spill."

No one could read me like Char. I both hated and loved that about her. At the moment I hated it. Gulping some more caffeine, I tried to act as nonchalant as possible by leaning my head on my right hand, and fiddling with the sugar bowl in the middle of the table. "He kinda gave me an orgasm."

"Mac! You better not be shitting me! This is insane! See, now do you understand what I'm telling you? The Man God is hot for you. Shit!" She clutched the edge of the table to keep herself in her seat. She looked like she wanted to get up on the table and twerk. "Tell me details! Tell me you flew to the stars! I need you to tell me that."

Char didn't exactly have an exciting life either at the moment, so hearing about my tryst would no doubt be the highlight of her day.

Recalling how Harley had dragged every ounce of pleasure from me had me grinning like a fool. "It was…incredible."

"God. He hasn't even dipped his dick in yet. Imagine what that will be like?"

"Charlotte! Can you not?"

My friend roared laughing, throwing her head back fully. I didn't find her humor funny at this point.

"Just saying." Checking her watch, she stood. "Gotta get back to it. Call me tonight if anything else happens." Blowing me an air kiss, she breezed out, leaving me with two minutes to get back to it. Confusion gripped me more than ever. Part of me wanted to throw caution to the wind and take a reckless chance on Harley, but I still had to deal with Nick, so I didn't need any other drama. For now I'd stick to my guns and send Harley on his way.

***

The rest of the day flew by and I couldn't help the flutter of anticipation in my belly at going home to the hunk of a man who'd be waiting. Tonight being our last night together, I would stop by the supermarket and get some fresh ingredients to cook him something special.

On my way down to the basement garage of the hospital, my cell pealed out. Checking the screen it read, Charlie. I didn't know anyone by that name. Unless…remembering the message I'd left when I'd called Harley's military buddy, I quickly answered. "Mackenzie speaking."

"Hi Mackenzie. It's Charlie O'Donnell. You called a couple of days ago. I've only just got back in the country. What can I do for you?"

His rich, husky voice befitted an armed forces soldier. "Hi Charlie. I'm a friend of Harley…uh Declan's. I needed to talk with you. Can you speak freely?"

"Yep. All good. Dec, huh? What's he up to since he's been home?"

"Ah. Well, here's the thing. He was shot and taken to hospital…"

"Son bitch! Is he okay? Did they catch the motherfucker who did it? Where is he now? I need to see him!"

Fury laced his words as he talked way too fast. I quickly replied before he could say anything else. "He's fine. He's out of hospital and has been staying at my place. I cared for him in ICU. Physically he'll make a full recovery, but he's got no memory prior to the shooting. He suffered head injuries when he collapsed."

"Jesus! I'm going to find out who did this and tear their head from their shoulders. What do you need from me? Anything. Name it."

I could already hear Charlie's loyalty to Harley. It pleased me they were close, and he had another ally, even if it were one-sided. "He won't remember you, so maybe just give him some space for now. Trudy is going to let him stay with her until the perpetrator is caught."

"Trudy? Ex-wife Trudy?" His voice turned bitter.

"Yeah."

"Oh, she's a piece of work that one."

"What do you mean?" My curiosity piqued.

"She's the reason they separated in the first place. Dec obviously doesn't remember, and I'm pretty sure she won't spill the beans."

Oh, this just got very interesting. Skeletons were coming out of the closet.

"Dec was away on missions a lot, like me, but Trudy knew his goals going in. Turns out, while he was away she was getting it on with Reno. You won't know Reno, but he went on a couple of missions with our team. He spent more time at home than us, so Trudy obviously took advantage of it."

Holy hell. Huge didn't cover it. I wonder if Harley ever found out. "Did Harley know about it?"

"He did when I found out and told him."

"How did you find out?" I submerged deeper into the story as more unfolded.

"I discovered a letter Reno had dropped. The last page was open on the floor of the rundown building we were holing up in. The words *always yours, Trudy* caught my eye, so I read the page and put two and two together. Trudy felt guilty and didn't want Dec to find out."

"Wow." I wasn't sure what else to say.

"Wow, is right. Dec freaked. At first he denied it, but when I told him I'd read the letter, he went apeshit. He threatened to kill Reno. He was going to confront him as soon as possible but he never got the chance."

"Reno was killed."

"How do you know this?" he barked.

"Declan had some memories in hospital about his friend's death."

"Reno was taken hostage while returning to our hideout. Dec was still pissed, but when he found out Reno had been captured, he did everything he could to save him. Put his anger aside. He was devastated when he couldn't save him."

"I can't believe this!"

"It is what it is. Now you know why Trudy isn't one of my favorite people."

"So what should I do? Let Declan go to her?"

"I wouldn't, but that's entirely up to you."

This changed everything. "Should I tell Declan,

seeing as though he has no memory of the affair?" Calling Harley, *Declan* made him a stranger to me, but I humored Charlie.

I heard him huff out. "Wouldn't hurt. Maybe if he can't recall it, he won't feel the same emotions attached to it."

Did Trudy have an agenda now? No doubt Harley losing his memory proved advantageous to her. She knew when she asked him to stay with her that she'd cheated on him. She must be very pleased with herself. All of a sudden, I saw her in a new light. How could she betray Harley the way she had? There's no way I could let him move in with her, knowing what I knew.

"Where do you live? I'm coming over?" His tone brooked no argument. It would be pointless in trying to dissuade him.

Giving him my address and telling him to leave it until eight p.m., I hung up and left the hospital to drive to the grocery store. My mind came alive with new thoughts.

One phone call had changed everything. I now believed Trudy wanted to get Harley back before he regained his full memory. How could she expect him to stay with her when he found out the truth?

I knew one thing for sure. Charlie could drop the bombshell again. He'd done it once. He'd do it again. I didn't want a part of it.

I picked up some salad ingredients to have with beef stroganoff. A quick and easy meal to prepare.

Driving home, I couldn't get Charlie's admission out of my mind. How had Trudy and Reno kept the affair silent? I guess it had been easy with Harley being away more than his comrade.

Things were getting messy. I'd pushed for Harley to get his memory back, but now I wasn't so sure it had been a great idea. Some things were better left forgotten. Still, running into Trudy had begun the unraveling of events, so I guess fate had won out. Nothing could have prevented it.

Parking my car in the garage, I got out, carrying the groceries.

Harley stood in the kitchen cleaning, much to my shock and gratitude. He had a cloth in one hand and cleaner in the other, and wiped down the counter tops. He looked up and smiled as I entered.

"Wow. This place looks amazing! I must say, it's a welcome sight to see a male doing chores." I laughed, placing the bags on the table.

"I like to earn my keep. I wasn't doing anything, anyway."

"I appreciate it."

"Do you want a hand putting those away?" He motioned to the groceries.

"Thank you. I've got a few things for dinner but I'll go grab a shower before I start." Should I mention Charlie's visit? Better to warn him. "I got a phone call today from someone you know."

"Oh?"

"Charlie O'Donnell."

It took a moment to register as his brain shuffled through the muck. Realization had him stand rigid. "How did he get your number?"

"Ah, Trudy gave it to me. I kinda called him."

Expecting him to be mad, he surprised me by walking to the cupboard under the sink and placing the cleaner and cloth inside. His shoulders relaxed. When he stood back up and faced me, he leaned his butt against the countertop. "And why would you call him?"

"To help solve the riddle that is you."

Smirking at me, he asked, "And what did Charlie have to say?"

Not wanting to give away anything, I replied, "I explained about your shooting and amnesia and he wanted to drop by. He's coming over at eight p.m. tonight. I hope you don't mind."

Rubbing the back of his neck, he puffed out, "He's game. I guess I don't mind, but it'll be a little awkward."

"That's why I bought this." I fished out a bottle of red wine from one of the bags.

Harley chuckled. "You think of everything, don't you?" He stepped toward me with purpose but I couldn't stick around. I needed that shower more than ever.

"I'll take that shower now. Can you finish putting these away?"

He stopped and frowned, nodding, his eyes revealing disappointment. God. I knew I teetered between hot and cold, but I didn't have a clue about anything when it came to Harley.

Standing under the warm spray only served to melt away a small percentage of tension in my muscles. I didn't really feel like having a visitor tonight. In fact, I wanted to down a glass of wine in my pajamas while watching television. With each second the shower spray pummeled me, fatigue took hold. We'd had two emergencies brought into the ICU back to back this afternoon and we'd been short staffed with two people calling in sick. Char and I had been run off our feet. Even with my expensive flats designed for people who stood on their feet all day, my calf muscles were tight and achy.

Perhaps when our guest arrived, Harley could serve the wine so I could put my feet up. I could only hope.

Drying off and donning a pair of lightweight sweatpants and a tee, I moved back into the kitchen. Another surprise. While I'd been indulging in the shower, Harley had prepared a large salad and went about finishing it off with some cashew nuts on the top. Damn, this man proved handy.

"Oh my God! You cook too?"

"I guess I do. I can't remember cooking, but I knew without a doubt how to throw a salad together. You like?"

Moving closer to look at the colorful masterpiece, I shrieked. "I love it! Thank you so much! I wonder what else you can do that you don't know about."

I hadn't meant it to sound sexual, but Harley took it that way, stepping into me and fingering my wet hair while leaning one hand on the table. "I know how to do this," he whispered, lifting my face with one hand. "And this." His lips found my forehead. A slow, soft kiss feathered my brow. "And I think I remember this from earlier." Dragging his mouth lightly down my nose, he sealed his lips over mine. It took my restraint away and eased the remaining tension the shower hadn't been able to.

Just a kiss, right? After the day I'd had, I needed something and this seemed to be working, even though I didn't want it to. Not really. Well, maybe a little.

He led and I followed. Gently as if I would break. It wasn't a full on snog but more of a lazy, *butterfly in the tummy* inducing slow dance. He hadn't kissed me this way before and I liked it. Unhurried and loving, as if we had all the time in the world. His chest beat heavily against mine. I opened my eyes and risked a peek. He'd plunged into the moment. Dense lashes brushed across his cheeks, lids lowered. I closed mine again, savoring the feel of him. The smell and taste. His tongue only served to sporadically search for mine, and each time they met it served more as a peck before he pulled it out again. It started to drive me insane. He knew how to lead, teasing me to want more. I did want more. So much more, but again I had to pull away.

"Harley. We need to finish dinner. It's nearly seven. Charlie will be here in an hour." My puffy lips made the words sound strange. Or maybe they were strange because they were the exact opposite of what I really wanted to say.

His face was a map of desire and I seriously wanted to dissolve into him but we couldn't.

Dropping his head for a moment and sucking in a deep breath, he nodded and managed to pull himself together, marginally. "Need a hand with the stroganoff?" I think he needed a distraction, but he'd already made the salad.

"No. I'll do it. You go shower if you want."

Running his index finger down my jawline, his eyes stuttered before he pulled himself away and left me alone.

Gah! That man! He'd truly rooted himself under my skin and I wasn't sure I could restrain myself anymore. Pouring us both a glass of wine and taking a healthy swig, I grabbed the pan out of the cupboard. After it heated I threw in the meat and seared it before adding the rest of the ingredients, allowing it to simmer for ten minutes. Removing it from the heat, I poured in the light sour cream at the end.

I hadn't heard the shower switch off, but Harley appeared a few minutes later dressed in a dark blue pair of jeans and a black Nike tee. Hot damn. The man filled out that shirt like nobody's business. The wine glass stopped mid-sip due to my shaking hand.

"Dinner smells amazing." He gifted me with a stunning smile. I had to put the glass down before I dropped it. Turning back to the pan, I lifted two plates down from the overhead cupboard. Piling on some stroganoff and salad, I handed him his plate and filled mine.

Sitting down together had an intimate feel, one I soaked in to my core. If and when Harley moved back to his apartment, I'd miss him. My decision to deter him from moving in with Trudy would wait until after Charlie broke the news. I was sure on hearing it, he wouldn't want to, anyway. Would he feel any betrayal or would the words wash over him like a light breeze? We'd soon find out.

"You're a great cook, you know that, right?"

Harley mumbled in between shoveling food into his mouth.

"Judging by the way your stashing that stroganoff away, it's either your favorite or maybe, and I'm stressing *maybe*, I'm an okay cook."

"Woman, stop selling yourself short." He paused before studying me. "Did Nick never tell you?"

"No," I whispered, realizing he never had. We barely ate together, and even if Nick had eaten his while poring over his computer on the rare occasion he came home when I ate, he'd never complimented me.

Loudly placing his fork down on his almost empty plate with a clatter, I raised my eyes to his.

"You're not seriously considering taking that asshole back, are you?"

"Wow! Say what you really think, Harley." I placed my own fork down somewhat quieter and took a sip of wine.

"It's true and you know it. He's all about himself. He can't see what's right in front of him. Take him back and nothing will ever change."

The truth glared at me. I didn't want Nick to even return to pick up the remainder of his stuff, but I knew he would in the hopes Harley had gone. He'd return any day now. At any given moment he could walk through the door. The idea of it soured my stomach.

Sighing out my agreement, I said, "He wasn't always bad. Not in the beginning."

As his jaw hardened, I cut him off, "But I have to agree. I need to let him go."

He relaxed at my statement. "I got your back,

okay?"

When I didn't immediately respond, he placed his large hand over my small one. "Hey. I'm here for you one hundred percent. The same way you have been for me. I promise."

I like hearing his vow of support. To have him swear his loyalty. Apart from my father, I hadn't had that, ever.

"Thank you." I smiled, genuinely grateful.

Suddenly remembering my request to have him call some security companies, I asked, "Did you find someone to come and fit an alarm?"

"Yep. I called four or five companies. Securaguard sounded the best in regards to the system for the price. They were fully booked until Wednesday, so I'll stay until then."

Relieved I'd soon have some protection and secretly cheering I'd have Harley for longer, I stood to clean up, noticing the time had gotten away. Charlie would be here soon and the kitchen needed tidying. "Thank you. I appreciate it."

"No drama. Now you go sit down. I'll clean. You've been on your feet all day."

My God. If he kept this up, I'd never let him go.

Following his advice, I took my refilled wine glass into the living room and settled in to await our visitor.

At exactly eight o' clock sharp a motorbike pulled into the driveway, followed by a loud rap on the door. Harley, who had joined me, found my gaze with a questioning look in his eyes. I nodded and he stood and walked to the door.

I wasn't surprised the guy standing outside

looked just as big as Harley, if not bigger. Height-wise, he appeared a tad shorter, but overall he reminded me of a tank. His short blond buzz cut and clean-shaven oval face were typical of a soldier, but his crystal blue eyes were in stark contrast to the rest of him. They were friendly eyes that crinkled at the corners as he held out his hand for Harley.

"Dec. Man. It's good to see you."

Harley stood statue-still, hands balled at his sides. Things were about to get real. I didn't know how the visit would go, but having someone else from his past appear hopefully meant more support for me while we dealt with Harley's amnesia. Everything had escalated quickly and skeletons were slowly being dragged out of the closet. I had a feeling the three of us were going to need each other more than we knew. For now I was happy to sit back and let Charlie take center stage.

END OF BOOK 1

Read on for a sneak peek at Book 2.

TRUE

SACRIFICE

Book Two of The Lost and Found Series

Chapter One

Harley

The guy standing in front of me grinned and held out a meaty hand for me to shake. Upon seeing his face, memories of my dream shot like adrenalin through my brain, triggering a fight or flight response. My body tensed as I processed the haphazard snapshots. Fighting. Brothers. Comradery. Loyalty. Fierce protection. Unspoken words. Instinct. An unbreakable bond, threatened by war. It all came hard and fast, slamming into me, causing me to step back. I continued to watch him. He continued to smile, his hand unwavering, waiting for me.

Clarity began sorting out the hazy muck as the first emotion since waking in the hospital bloomed in my heart. This guy meant everything to me. He'd had my back without question, and vice-versa. Till the death. Details eluded me, but the knowing he'd die for me was absolute.

Regaining my composure and standing taller, a

small smirk played at the edges of my mouth, which until now had been set in a flat line.

Feelings swelled, the tide of my blood carrying them through my body. They seeped into the black crevices formed by amnesia.

Letting the smile engulf my face and surging forward, I embraced my best friend in a powerful hug, clapping him on the back, overcome with emotion. Tears beckoned, but I held them at bay as I swallowed hard and winced. My gunshot wound protested the gesture, but I ignored it, not giving a shit about physical pain, because to finally feel the connection of someone other than Mac, a person from my past, overrode all else.

"Viper." Nothing else came out. We pulled back and scrutinized each other. His blond buzzed hair sprouted from his scalp like new grass. Clean-shaven face. Blue eyes held mischief complementing the dimple on his left cheek.

"What's this bullshit about you not remembering me?" he balked.

I moved away from him, motioning for him to enter. His eyes fell on Mac and then returned to me. An eyebrow rose in question.

Shutting the door, I found Mac intensely focused on both of us, her face lit with joy at our exchange.

She stood before I could answer my friend and came to greet him.

"Hi. I'm Mac. We spoke on the phone."

Viper's eyes mapped her out. Assessing. Ogling. It took a moment for him to respond as he held out his hand. "Call me Viper."

She nodded. "Please sit."

We took our places, me beside Mac in some territorial display of ownership. Viper sat on the single recliner beside us.

"So are you gonna answer me, douche?" Viper laughed.

His banter wasn't offensive. In fact, it settled me. Much like Mac's presence. My subconscious knew.

"I don't remember much at all. Seeing you though, it triggered the memory I had of us in Afghanistan. The day Reno…"

I stopped short upon seeing Viper's face scrunch and his eyes briefly flit to Mac before he cracked his neck and focused on me again.

"Sorry, man. I shouldn't have brought him up."

"Don't worry about it. We both lost a friend that day." He shifted uncomfortably.

Mac rose to offer drinks. "Wine, Viper? Harley and I were having a couple before you arrived."

His face twitched as he acknowledged Mac. "Wine sounds good. I'd prefer beer, but I'll take what I can get." Turning back to me, he chuckled. "Harley, huh? That will take a bit of getting used to. Are you going to have everyone call you that?"

"Yep. It's who I am now. I associate myself with him."

"Fair enough. I'll call you whatever you want. I'm just glad you're alive."

"You and me both, although waking up with no past leaves a lot to be desired."

"Any idea who shot you?" Viper asked, taking the glass from Mac before she sat down and handed me my refill.

"Terrorist. I'm certain. A snippet of that night

came to me. I chased a lead on a planted explosive in a nightclub in town. Everyone evacuated. I searched in an alley. It's where the police found me. There's nothing after that."

"Hmm. It's possibly connected to the cell who captured and killed Reno. We killed their leader. Could be personal now."

Forcing out air, I sensed Mac's fear beside me. Her quiet curse and nervous shifting gave her away. Without looking, I squeezed her leg. It comforted me as well.

The thought of having a target on my back didn't sit well, and I sure as hell didn't want her involved.

We'd discussed me moving in with my ex-wife Trudy, who lived in a secure estate to offer some protection. Mac had insisted, even though I knew her heart said otherwise. Now, it seemed like I didn't have a choice.

Spinning around, I caught the worry swimming in her eyes, but it was a small price to pay to keep her safe. "I'm gonna move in with Trudy as planned. I don't want you involved in any of this shit. I mean it, Mac. I'll do whatever it takes to protect you."

Her frown deepened as her head fell downwards, eyes focused on her lap.

"Ah, man, you may want to consider moving in with me instead." Reno's voice had taken on a rough edge.

Standing, I walked over to the living room window, not to look out, but to give myself something to do because I sensed a missile about to hit its target.

Without turning, I asked, "Why is that, Viper?"

Silence. Patience wore thin as each second ticked by with no answer.

Turning, I caught the end of a stolen glance between Viper and Mac. A secret.

"What's going on?" I held my ground, steadying myself for whatever came.

"Ah, man. I've already told you this once and it was hard back then. To have to do it again is killing me. I'm just the messenger, okay? So don't shoot me."

My blood thickened, slowing down my heartrate to almost nothing as I held my breath.

I glared at him, unable to utter a sound. Whatever he needed to get off his chest weighed a ton. His shoulders sagged.

"The reason you and Trudy split up is because you found out she had been having an affair."

Spine fully extending, I soaked in the words. My wife had cheated? A small sense of betrayal dug a hole in my chest, but nothing major with no recollection of it. More like my pride was bruised hearing it from my friend. And then Mac sat in the room, anxiously watching on, twirling her wine glass but not drinking.

"Oh? And you know how?" It didn't really matter, but I wanted to know.

"I found a letter while on deployment. It was from Trudy."

Confusion had me stare into space to debunk the riddle. How would a letter from my wife get into a war zone without me knowing? Unless…

Betrayal had me thunder across the carpet,

pointing a finger. "You son bitch! You fucked my wife?" How could he enter my home all brotherly and drop that whopper on me?

Standing, he lifted both hands to placate me. "Easy, big fella. Not me."

The relief only lowered slightly. "If not you, who?"

Would I even remember the guy's name?

Viper's features took on an anguished guise. He eyeballed me directly and uttered the one word I never would have guessed.

"Reno."

About the Author

I am married and a mother of two beautiful children, living in sunny Queensland, Australia. I've been reading books ever since I can remember and love all things related to books. Writing has become an extension of that and I hope to pursue a full time writing career. I currently write part-time and work as a remedial massage therapist. I love spending time with family and hope to one day travel to Italy and England.

Facebook:
https://www.facebook.com/amandamackeyauthorpage

Twitter:
https://twitter.com/AmandaMacey43

Website:
http://amandamackeyauthor.com/

Goodreads:
https://www.goodreads.com/author/show/7069947.Amanda_Mackey